T0381460

BEHIND THE VEIL

CHRIS AIKOSHORIA OMIYI

authorHOUSE®

AuthorHouse™ UK
1663 Liberty Drive
Bloomington, IN 47403 USA
www.authorhouse.co.uk
Phone: UK TFN: 0800 0148641 (Toll Free inside the UK)
*   UK Local: (02) 0369 56322 (+44 20 3695 6322 from outside the UK)*

Published by AuthorHouse 07/27/2023

ISBN: 979-8-8230-8403-1 (sc)
ISBN: 979-8-8230-8404-8 (e)

Print information available on the last page.

This book is printed on acid-free paper.

CONTENTS

PROLOGUE

One day she is a child, the next day she is a forced bride. Brutal reality of many under-aged children of the female gender in Africa with majority coming from Nigeria. Voiceless victims of stolen innocence and then abandoned to suffer the consequence, Viscos Vaginal Fistula, while others are left vulnerable for human trafficking.

Infant male, called **Almajiri**, intentionally abandoned by parents, scorned by society and abused by politicians. Born to suffer, denied of parental love at infancy, taken to unknown destination far from his place of birth to be religiously indoctrinated at childhood; given a plate as tool for survival to beg for alms to survive, then gets above the age of begging to survive, for lack of nothing to do, takes his destiny in his hand, reluctantly throws the plate away and overnight turns into a beast with gun in his quiver. A bandit and violent criminal!

The summary of their lives is thus 'childhood a mistake, adulthood a struggle, old age a regret.'

This book is a true story chronicling the societal

atrocities meted against the girl child who becomes a bride as early as eight years old and the young boys who are left to fend for themselves as soon as they begin to walk. Nigeria, the largest country in Africa, has the largest number of child brides and abandoned boys. The practice is most prevalent in the predominantly Muslim north where conservative Islamic groups and the state legislators staunchly resist efforts to criminalize child marriage and the infant male, popularly called Almajiri, who are left to fend for themselves beginning from the age of four. An obviously evil system created to refuse and smash the innocent male children of their childhood. These practices are justified by cultural beliefs instigated by the myopic and uninformed position of religion. When evil hides behind tradition, culture and religion, things get complicated and extremely difficult to correct, and then things fall apart and the centre cannot hold. It is a cultural manipulation wrapped under religious ambience, holding strong to nonsensical traditions in conflict with modernity which puts the female gender in perpetual servitude and bondage.

Behind the veil is a book with sordid tale of the creation of Almajiri system. A system that deliberately creates a class of people denied of moral instructions, persuaded to use violence as a means of resolving differences, denied of education, born without parentage and put on the street to beg for alms without any emotional attachment to family, loyal to no system but a defender of a long outstanding trading of begging for their uninformed teachers.

Behind the veil also gives experiential exposure of sex slave and human trafficking of Nigerian ladies, majorly in Libya and Europe.

I see many evil in the land of AFRICA, but four evils irk me the most. First is child marriage, second is the Almajiri system, third is woman trafficking for sex slavery, and fourth is banditry created by the system itself– the harbinger of poverty. This is the face of BEHIND THE VEIL.

CHAPTER ONE

Agony at its peak

It was twenty minutes past the hour of fifteen on a very sunny Monday afternoon. The average temperature of the sun is 42 degree Celsius, so many school children were walking bare footed on the undulating dusty road leading to the main market. Behind the main market is a residential quarter, the actual destination of the school children. The residences are shanties scattered carelessly with no particular formation and heaps of dirt makes the sign post for the quarters, one of the largest slums in the vicinity. Among these students trekking under the unfriendly sun is Fatima Garuba, a prodigious child, and even the best brain the community school has ever seen. Her house stands gallantly beside the slum adjacent to the main market.

The shanties

Few minutes later, Fatima, the twenty -seventh child of Mallam Abdullah Garuba galumphed into the compound, with pain written all over her face. She saw her father pointed to her and telling the visitors with pride,

'That is the girl. A ripe one as you can see!'

He spoke rapidly in the native Hausa language. Fatima, pretending not to have heard him, greeted everybody and went into her room, hoping it was not what she was thinking.

"Hope these people have not come here for any marriage rubbish talk", she thought within herself. Her worst fear is marrying as a child; the fear which grows rapidly in her mind, caused by series of ugly experiences from her immediate family and neighbors. Her best friend and elementary school mate, Aisha, an extremely brilliant girl like her, who followed Fatima behind in class positions. While the former would always have the second or third position, the latter would, without doubt always come out first. On one Monday morning, "A dry one", as Fatima would always bitterly recollect, the news filtered into the classroom that Aisha would not be coming to school again because she got married the previous Friday. The news spread round the school like wild fire causing seizure of pains on the students, especially her friends. Aisha was only eleven years old when she was forced into marriage. All her hopes of a good life was tied to the whims and caprices of her husband who was 57 years old. The major catalyst of her forced marriage was humiliating poverty which was an aftermath of her father marrying so many women he could not afford to take care of.

When she asked her mother about school, and pouring out her desire to excel in her academics and her aspiration and dreams to become a lawyer, the mother solemnly replied,

'The same man who will marry you will take you to school.'

But when she got married, she was denied her right to education. It became an imposed duty to take care of her husband, something she never bargained for. Fatima could not fathom how an eleven year old girl, an intimate friend and classmate, a small girl like Aisha will take care of a fifty seven year polygamist and a pedophile.

Aisha's mother, on her part, nurtured her pain to herself. She was perplexed, she dared not speak out against the practice. She was only burdened in her heart that her baby daughter who can hardly take care of herself will be having new responsibilities as a wife. Sadly and amazingly, she discovered that few months into the marriage, her daughter was pregnant. She was hurt when she discovered she was pregnant, at least the husband would have waited a little for the young Aisha to mature. Her daughter has joined the league of motherhood. Aisha, like her mother, has become a victim. A victim of forced marriage and motherhood at an unripe age. What a vicious circle. Like her daughter,

Aisha's mother remembered how she suffered the same fate, how she had no interest in marriage at that time. An innocent child who was very studious, hoping that one day she would become a medical doctor. She had wanted to achieve her dreams before marriage would come into view but her father forcedly sold her off to a man too old to be her father. Her father, an Imam, insisted she must marry a man she never met before and of course she was nervous and scared. She cried her way to her new home because she was too tender to experience the abandonment of her parents and did not know where she was being taken to. She remembered she got married sixteen years ago. She thinks she was fifteen; she didn't know her husband's age. 'Had she been given the privilege to speak, she would have begged her father to give her the grace to graduate from post-primary school before he gave her to the man, her said husband.

'Hmm… Aisha is too young,' she would constantly say to herself. Now it's no longer her fate but her daughter's.

'One thing I secretly used to think is that our life would change for the better when Aisha married Alhaji Haruna. Now even the dream that I had that my other children would live a good life is turning out to be a myth. Is my hope for Aisha's marriage not shattered?'

To her, marrying out Aisha at eleven years was bad but getting pregnant was even abominable. Many things ran through her mind, she could not imagine how a child will give birth to a child. How will her infantile body adjust to pregnancy? She silently prayed for her child's protection against Viscose Vaginal Fistula. When she shared her fears concerning the consequences of being pregnant at that age to Aisha's uneducated father, he responded harshly,

'Woman, do you think that man bought her for a piece of furniture?'

He continued with his unguided talk,

'Any girl that is married must get pregnant no matter the age. You better understand that Aisha is gone for good and praise be to Allah that is one less mouth to feed!'

Aisha's mum tried to control her bitterness. She had always feared and respected her husband but this time she was enraged and didn't know when she raised her voice at him,

"But you promised her that she would continue her education even after she is married. Now that she is pregnant, don't you know that that pregnancy is a major obstacle between Aisha and her education? At this delicate age, how is she supposed to handle that small thing in her belly, not to talk of accepting womanhood!"

Her husband looked at her irritatingly,

'You *Tsohuwa, who told you that rubbish! Oh, I can see that you are now listening to what school people tell you. And when did you start raising your voice at me?'

Aisha's mother left him with tears.

For Fatimah, her mind still brought sad stories of child marriage she had had from several people. She remembered a case of a neighbour, Halima, whose father refused her of going to school because he thought it was a waste of time and money to sponsor a girl child to school. Will she not return to the kitchen even if she gets educated?

Halima was later forced into marriage at the age of nine and got pregnant a year later. Unfortunately for the poor girl she lost the baby as a result of some complication in child birth. As if that was not enough, she became diagnosed with *Eclamsia and Puerperal endometritris*.

Fatimah also remembered another terrible case of one thirteen year old. The girl was well known in her community having won several local awards in junior science competitions. Halima tried to escape when she discovered that her father was planning to give her hands in marriage to one seventy-one year old man. Her escape attempt failed, and at the order of her father, was beaten to stupor until she passed away. It became a secret case and never allowed into the public.

The story of Aisha and Mariam and other girls put all her schoolmates in deep fear and never wish that they will find themselves in such cases. While her mates were in school, Aisha spent most of the time in the kitchen cooking for her husband who insisted that she cooked regardless of her inexperience in cooking.

There are many Aishas in Nigeria with buried dreams and lost potentials. Imagine a female child at a very tender age put into marriage- the aftermaths are always degrading. The victims eventually become physically and mentally imbalanced apart from putting their health into jeopardy. When the issue of forced marriage is discussed among themselves, Fatima and her friends had already decided on what to do. They resolved to resist being married as kids no matter the oppression and force from their parents. For Fatima this is a battle between life and death.

The story of little Rukiya, another victim of forced and early marriage, is very pathetic. Since she was three, her father has been telling her she belongs to the kitchen and 'the other room.' She is currently nine years old and never allowed to see the four walls of a class room. It was pitiable when she was introduced to a man of sixty-nine years as her husband. The first night of the marriage, the old man took a sex enhancement drug and forced himself on the little girl until the man had cardiac arrest and he passed away. Little Rukiya was later labeled a witch, beaten to stupor by the relatives of the husband not minding the pains she underwent due to the injuries she encountered from the forced intercourse. She was later expelled from the community and stigmatized as a husband killer.

Subsequently, some parts of Nigeria is predominantly a patriarchal society, making it extremely difficult for girls to acquire secondary or tertiary education, or aspire for high positions in government or the corporate sector.

A girl child below the age of puberty or below the legal age of adulthood is subjected to this treatment because of the stupidity of a man old enough to be her grandfather.

Fatimah also taught of Mamuna who was forced into child marriage at the age of eleven years. Mamuna, like the other girls, was a brilliant child with promising future. Pitifully, her academic and vocational pursuits were brought into abrupt end by forced marriage and early pregnancy which resulted in her social isolation. Mamuna also became a victim of domestic violence. A day hardly went by that her cry would not be heard in the community. She never did anything right as far as her husband was concerned. He had a permanent whip he used to flog her. Sores resulting from whip lash all over her body until she had a life threatening illness. Due to superstition and belief that Mamuna was being punished by God for resisting her husband, no serious attention was paid to her ailments which included Viscose-Vaginal Fistula VVF), Anemia, and High Blood Pressure (HBP). She also suffered from malnutrition, Sexually Transmitted Diseases (STDs) and Postpartum Depression (PPD). She would have succeeded in her suicide attempts if not for the always timely intervention of her husband's third wife, who also got married at an early age of fifteen. This young woman also has serious resentment for child marriage and wouldn't give her consent to it. Mamuna became her favourite among her husband's wives majorly because they were both victims of early marriage.

Fatimah's father's comments brought back the memories of her discussion with her teacher. When she asked her teacher, "Ma, what is the meaning and causes of Fistula?"

The teacher was taken aback.

'Why did you ask?' she asked.

Fatimah told her she heard about it killing some young girls. The teacher looked at her tenderly and said, 'I'll tell you all about it, dear,' she said, and beckoned to Fatima to sit next to her.

'It's reportedly one of the worst epidemics predominantly caused by early child birth. An obstetric fistula is a hole between the vagina and rectum or bladder that is caused by prolonged obstructed labor, leaving a woman incontinent of urine and or faeces. Over time, it leads to chronic medical problems like frequent infections, kidney disease and infertility. Medically, when an under-aged girl has sex, gets pregnant and goes through childbirth, because her body is not developed enough for child bearing, she is highly exposed to a fistula.'

This explanation created great fear in Fatimah and she vowed that she would rather die than to marry at a too tender age.

Salamatu who was another victim of child marriage lost all hopes of becoming a medical doctor she had always aspire for. She would work extremely hard at school especially in the elementary science subjects and would come out top beating all her classmates to a distant second position.

One sad Tuesday afternoon, the father told her she cannot continue with school because one of the prominent politicians was coming for her hand in marriage the next Friday. Salamatu was just fourteen. She looked at her father with tears and asked soberly,

'How about my dream of becoming a doctor, Papa?' Her father replied in a very affirmative tone,

'Daughter, not all dreams come true in life.'

The dreaded Friday came and the marriage was elaborately celebrated as there were people of high statuses that attended. Little did the public know that tragedy was lurking at the corner. A day after the marriage, Salamatu's husband invited some of his best friends' home for dinner. Salamatu poisoned the food and all except one of them died. All attempts to revive them by the doctor was futile. She was arrested by the police and after several interrogation by the local Police, she confessed guilty of the offence. She said she was forced into marriage and even to a man old enough to be her grandfather. Instead of trying her at the juvenile court of law, Salamatu was tried at an adult court. The government officials who took her to court insisted that any married lady is an adult and not a child. The human right group advocated for her that she must be treated as a child and solicited for international collaborators to bring to the public this heinous crime against the girl child. She was later discharged and acquitted when the situation was becoming an embarrassment to the government but this incident never became an instrument to put an end to the practice of child marriage.

Fatimah's mind also flashed on twelve years old Nnali. She was a quiet, beautiful and humble girl and one of the best behaved children of Umar Mustapha. On one early morning, Umar Mustapha called the twelve years old Nnali and told her,

'From tomorrow you will be going to a new home as your home.' He was sending her to live with a man of sixty-seven years old. Although this was a common practice, Umar Mustapha did feel downcast about giving the small girl to an old man. He thought, 'Kai, Walahi, it would have been reasonable if the husband was between the range of fifty and fifty-five years old.' He considered this not because of the wellbeing of his daughter but because he felt that death was still far from a fifty-five year old man than that of a sixty-seven. However, the offer of the sixty-seven years old man was totally irresistible and he was also a very influential person in the society. He is one of the richest farmers in the community hence the dowry was like an open cheque to Umar Mustapha, Nnali's father. The dowry consisted of some kola nuts (native to the African tropics), three cows, sewing machine and a pledge to be totally responsible for Umar Mustapha's medical bills and feed allowance. Offers like this are very rare, and the beauty of little Nnali was so arresting that they hardly waited for her to grow. When she was 8 years old, the father was to marry her out to the same man but for the intervention of Mother Nature. The mother of Nnali fell sick mysteriously over the taught of sending away her little 8 years daughter to an old man. This retarded Umar Mustapha's action at that time, but this time the economic situation of his family compelled the mother to simmer down and allow Nnali to be the scape goat. In trying to convince Nnali's mother, Umar Mustapha opined,

'This is what happens when a girl reaches puberty. It is our culture. Every family practices it, and we cannot be different. If we keep Nnali to grow older it will be difficult to get a suitor. But now that she is getting married early, she will grow rapidly and learn how to take care of a man and the home and bring honor to her family.

'As a father, you have to do what is best for your family. If your daughter is ready for marriage, you do what you must to make sure she finds a good man.'

Despite the consequences of underage marriage which stare the people in the face, the practice is still happily practiced by many of their men, especially their imams and pilgrims, in these northern parts of the country. Most of the under aged marriage is a living hell characterized with abuse. The underage brides are forced to conform or in extreme cases are divorced.

Halimatu, Nnali's cousin, who was barely fifteen years old was already a divorcee at the age of twelve. One of her father's friends came to the house and asked for a bride among the fathers five daughters and she was the eldest and being the eldest, her father instructed to marry his friend but she protested openly in front of the suitor this angered her father so much that he flogged her until she submitted to the demand. Her dream of being a lawyer was automatically truncated. She went to her husband house with very deep rooted bitterness that plagued the marriage. She wanted to continue her education but the husband vehemently opposed it. When he was going to work, he locked her in the house hence the problem became worse because Halimatu was fond of reading books but this did not go down well with the husband. One day, he came home and found out she was reading a storybook and he got really angry and beat her. He said a wife's place is in the house not at school. He was abusive and demanded sex every evening. Halimatu could not take it anymore. She knew she had to fight for her life or she would lose it. She started a habit of deliberately disrespecting the husband as a way of escaping the traumatic ordeal. The husband became very angry and threw her out of the house. She ran home to her mother and begged not to be returned to her husband. Her angry husband divorced her immediately and threw all her properties outside, neighbors tried to intervene to resolve the difference but it failed woefully.

Her father was very angry and embarrassed. There was no reason good enough for a wife to disrespect her husband. He threatened to kill her but her mother and other elders of the family pleaded on her behalf. He stopped talking to her because he believed she brought shame to the family. He disowned her. Halimatu has since gone back to school, to avoid a situation where other young brides will adopt her style she was sent away to another city to stay with her maternal aunt. Her situation became better especially because she wasn't pregnant. She had taken her studies very seriously with the hope of being a lawyer one day and fight this child marriage. Her friend who was in similar situation with no education or prospects of finding a job, roamed the streets almost bare footed selling bean cake and mobile phone vouchers. The travail of Halimatu's friend had re-enforced the impact of the practice of child marriage as it negatively affects both individual and the societal levels and it is therefore imperative in exacerbate poverty and subsequently promote economic degradation. No other singular factor affects the potential of young girls like child marriages and also have an adverse impact on the economy by eradicating opportunities for career and vocational advancement for young girls, because once they are trapped in the horrific circle of child marriage, their life is set on auto-reverse. It therefore disempowers women and stifles the prosperity of a country because when a significant number of the workforce is rendered economically inactive, the nation will suffer due to lost potentials. Its health implications are just as dire. There are several health risks that these young girls are exposed to. Most of them get pregnant at an age where normal vaginal births are difficult because their hips are not wide enough for the baby to be pushed through the vaginal canal and this can lead to the death of the mother and the baby. Also, the babies are exposed to diseases due to the lack of micronutrients in the girl's body and most babies do not survive this case. Halimatu had vowed to put her life on the line to end child bride. She felt like a conqueror for successfully sabotaging her own marriage. She made the marriage a living hell for the husband and she has adopted it as one of her strategies. Halimatu believed that the fundamental and root cause of sending children to marry men old enough to be their grandfather is poverty, nothing but abject poverty! She noticed that it was only the poor that gave off their female child to marriage. This, they believe, is part of the survival strategy of most poor families. One of the most attractive elements of the bride price is the cow most families look forward to owing their own cows. Secondly, the earlier they send the girls away, the less mouth they have to feed. In many of these communities, a family's wealth is measured in terms of the herd of cattle they own and young girls are the medium of payment. Most of these rural dwellers are not too happy with their wives if they don't give birth to female.

In her little way Halimatu has been posing an obstruction to child marriage based on her experience, she has been preaching resistance and defiance to the little girls she has a friend in her neighborhood called Rikiya. They used to play and study together, her dreams is to be a doctor, very intelligent and bright, in view of many abandoned child brides suffering from fistula, she has several people close to her in that condition of broken humanities, smelling and stigmatized while the men who put them in that condition had taken up new brides.

One bright cool evening as Halimatu and Rikya who just turned 13 years returned from school, there was a gathering in Rikiya family's house. Different types of vehicles littered the compound and the adjoining road. Well-dressed police men were there in their numbers; some directed the traffic while others were providing security for the big occasion. A big and rich politician is involved. Rikiya's family and relative were fully involved in the celebration. She was taken aback. Her mother came in suddenly, looking stressed out,

'Rikiya, please go and get prepared. You are marrying today.'

'MARRY?' Rikiya retorted and started crying, 'How can I marry a man I have not met!'

The marriage was a sole decision of her father. Her mind flashed immediately to her dream of becoming a doctor. *God...* this will be a big loss for her as she had a vision for a better life. It is a lost opportunity for her community considering the number of doctors in the northern part of the country. Looking very confused, Halimatu gave a loud cry.

Unless serious action is taken to end child marriage, many young women will follow a similar way and loss their God given dreams, this remains one of the major obstacles to the country's social and economic development.

Halimatu turned to Rikiya,

'Your cries will fall on deaf ear, you have to take

your destiny in your hand, if you marry that old man you are ruined but if you run away you may survive to tell the story one day.'

'Where will I run to,' Rikiya asked with desperation.

'Just run to anywhere,' Halimatu replied.

Like a possessed lady, Rikya went into the room. Her mother, on seeing her, taught she was going to get ready for the marriage, but unknown to them, Rikiya, took a small bag and ran through the back door into thin air. All the guest and the old groom waited until it became very obvious the marriage would not hold because of the disappearance of the bride. This was strange in this community. Fingers started pointing at Halimatu, who had a sense of victory.

Halimatu continued her war against child marriage with the caption silencing the wedding bells with resilience and disobedience. She gathered young girls who were on their way to or from schools, and gave them pep talk on how defiled the authorities concerning child marriage is, 'If they force you to go to the man's house, start misbehaving and make the marriage miserable. If they plan your marriage and you get a hint of it, runaway even if you have nowhere to go. On the wedding day when the guest are arriving, don't beg, don't cry. Fight for your dreams. Stand your ground. One day they will stop.' This message was impacting on the young girls.

One of the young girls Halimatu strongly impacted by her indoctrination is Binta. She became a potent demonstration of this indoctrination and mindset change. Binta was fourteen years and hoped to serve her community as a medical doctor in the future. About nine months ago her dream of creating positive impact were sidetracked when her father unilaterally declared he was marrying her off. Her husband to be was a sixty-one year-old man who was four times older than her. Her bride price was set at three white Fulani cows, fifty litres of groundnut oil, various food stuff and of course huge sum of money. She resisted the marriage but was eventually forced to go to the man's house against all advice from the head master of the school educating the father of the huge potentials his daughter possesses. After spending some weeks in the husband's house where she was sexually violated and physically abused, Binta's resilience was further fueled when she saw Halimatu again. Binta managed to escape one night due to what Halimatu had been telling her. She knew where to run to and get help.

Halimatu had been able to garner subtle support from older women who were once victims, whose dreams to good life was aborted at infancy by child marriage and managed to survive the system. One of such women is a forty- five-year-old mother of seven called Shannon. She was very brilliant in school but her father insisted she must leave school and marry a man sixty years older than her. Although he was a strong man but the man died ten years after the marriage, in that ten years she was able to give birth to seven children. After the man died, they wanted her to marry another man but she vehemently refused opting for business. She was very industrious and creative in view of her very high intelligent quotient.

'I will never let any of my daughters get married before they finish university. My time is over but my children will have a better future. The medical doctor I was deprived of becoming at least two of my girls will be medical doctors.'

She has been receiving help from donor agencies and NGOs.

CHAPTER TWO

Follies in families

The next morning, Fatima was getting ready for school when the father sent the mother to tell her to wait for the visitors who were coming. The same visitors that came some days ago, had started to arrive, this time in larger number. Fatima looked at her mother curiously, 'Mama, what do they want and why must I wait for them?'

The mother looked away with tears in her eyes not wanting to let the cat out of the bag. "My daughter, you will understand very soon just be patient," she replied calmly with her head turned away from her daughter.

'Understand what?' Fatima retorted.

It dawned on her what was about to befall her. Her mind flashes through all the stories of child marriages she had heard about. She remembered vividly the case of Aisha, her friend and school mate. It was always the centre of discussion in her class. Fatima knew this was the best time to move or forever be caged in a marriage she did not want.

She moved outside the house through the back door unnoticed, frowning as the mid- morning sun hit her slightly in the face partly covered by her blue nylon Hijab. She slipped from her shoes and stocking while trying to maneuver the big trees at the back of the house. As she moved towards the road, she could see more of the guest arriving the house, some sixty yards off from the house, Fatimah stopped and turned facing the direction of the house. Suddenly, the rest of the world felt so far away from her. The dice is cast, there was no turning back, only death will bring her back to that house. She looked at the house for the last time and she started to walk away hurriedly, her mind heaving. She walked over 30km to the only place she knew she might find help. She was stressed out and scared. Her feet were dusty and swollen due to the long distance she had walked.

Dr. Amina Yaro was surprised to see her at that time of the day and looking so worn out. He helped her into the house,

'Rest my child,' she said motherly, handling her a cup of water.

Fatimah looked into thin air, totally lost in thought.

Dr. Amina Yaro has been a crusader against child marriage, a respected child right activist in the northern part of Nigeria. She was a victim of child marriage. After breaking herself free from the scourge, she got a scholarship to study law abroad. On her return to the country as a trained lawyer, she started educating young girls on the need to take their destiny in their hands when it comes to child marriage. Many victims of child marriage have been rescued by her and given a new lease of life although with high resistance from the parents and family members of the victims. She visits schools under the guise of carrier counselling before the school authorities realizes her mission to the schools. It was on one of such visits she met Fatima who was highly indoctrinated by her teaching. Many of the conservatives believe she is a bad influence on their daughters thus fueling rebellion.

'I don't like what your parents are making you to pass through. It's totally not fair,' Dr. Amina spoke to Fatima in cool consoling voice.

There was no response from Fatima who was still trying to recuperate from the hassles she has just been through. She was staring into the thin air in the expanse living room.

The day moved by quickly in Malllam Abdullah Garuba's house, Fatima's father, as Fatima's suitor and his family members were soon arriving in their numbers for the marriage introduction. Mallam Abdullah, Fatima's father, found himself wishing his daughter, Fatima would just come in. By the time it was evening, Mallam Abdullah was pacing like a caged lion beholding its prey but restricted by the impregnable iron cage.

'Hajia, where is your daughter, Fatima?' he pounced at Fatima's mother.

'I have sent people to look for her in the school,' she replied with panic in her voice.

'You mean to tell me that nobody saw Fatima leaving this house after I told you to inform her not to go anywhere today?'

'I'm sorry my husband. After I told her there was no school for her today, I went into the kitchen to prepare food for our visitors. I did not know she will disobey our instruction. She has always been a good girl, you know.'

After scrutinizing the house, Mallam Abdullah's eyes rested on Fatima's school bag lying carelessly on the corridor leading outside the house from the back door. He hastened to the back door behind the house where an elderly woman in her late sixties runs a provision store. He usually thought her senseless about her indifference to the happenings in the neighborhood as a man holding a straw to survive. He curiously enquired about his daughter from her,

'Why do you want to destroy this young girl? The best brain her school has ever produced?' she retorted, and not waiting for any response from him, she continued,

'Because of ignorant men like you who force underage children to marry, our hospital is filled with children suffering from Fistula.'

Mallam Abdullah did not bargain for this. He became restless. His visitors are waiting in the sitting room and here is a woman talking to him rudely. As he tried to walk away, the woman held his shirt and looked at him straight in the eyes,

'Once a fistula is formed, fecal or urinary incontinence and peroneal nerve palsy may result and this may lead to humiliation, ostracism, and resultant depression. Most of these girls that pass through such are unable to live a normal life again.'

She paused to let her message sink, and then continued,

'Can you hear me? You are subjecting your child to a lot of health risk, such as sexually transmitted diseases, cervical cancer and so on.'

Mallam Abdullah could no longer tolerate her affront, he jerked his hand off her grip and walked straight to the visitors. He was scared of looking at the groom who sat with disdain at a corner of the room. He however managed to address them,

'I am afraid to tell you that something serious has happened...'

He stopped abruptly, thinking the guest would ask what has gone wrong but none of them seemed interested to hear him as they had all perceived the dreaded thing had happen.

He cleared his throat,

'I cannot find my daughter!'

There was a disturbed silence. Suddenly the brother of the proposed groom sprang up, poking a finger to Mallam Abdullah, shouted,

'I don't think this is fair on us. Walahi Mallam, *baka tarbiyyantar da 'yarka da kyau!'

Mallam Abdullah, surprised by the response, said,

'I expect you to understand. You know my travail

25

has just started, I am thinking of how to get my daughter back from whoever has encamped her.'

Mallam Abdullah Garuba, Fatima's father, was a petty trader who lived in the ancient city of Kano. He had four wives which he believed to be religiously right. However, since religion restricts him to marry not more than four wives, he acquires more concubines. Despite that he earns a meagre salary of thirty thousand naira every month, he aspired for more children to the already thirty-seven children he has.

Guest still troop into the compound but they are all soon disappointed when they see that the bride has run away. Among the arriving guest, in his Prado jeep, is the chairman of the local council, Alhaji Musa. He was finally able to get to Mallam Abdulla's house after the delay by hanger-on and praise singers on the road. They wouldn't leave him until he gave them money. As he alighted from his car, a health worker he knew way back in school met him and they exchanged pleasantry. The attention of the health worker was drawn to some of the children in the compound with a deformity of the polio virus.

'Chairman,' he called, pointing to the deformed children.

'What are you doing about these children?' the chairman frowned,

'What do you want me to do? Am I the person that caused the deformity? Don't call my attention to this nonsense again, please.'

The health worker was taken aback confirming the notion in his mind that the politicians are callous and care less about the people they represent. How can the people's representative be a guest of honor in an underage marriage when he was supposed to fight against it? The chairman of the local government area who is supposed to be closer to the people is nonchalant and indifferent to the people's plight. The local government is supposed to be the third tier of government designed to provide basic amenities to the rural populace such as health centers, primary schools, water and many other basic needs but he can see that the reverse is the case here. The local government only puts in so much energy collecting taxes and levies from the poor people. The schools are dilapidated; the roads are terribly bad such that cars cannot be driven to the areas. Many car owners have resorted to hiring motor cycles to traverse the road. Apart from levy and taxes, the local government gets revenue from the federal government and the whole money is shared by the politicians at the expense of the people they govern. This vividly explains part of the reasons for high level of poverty and underdevelopment.

The health worker gave a wry smile and apologized frantically to the chairman very well aware of the implication of being in the bad book of the chairman in a society like this where there are no values. Sadly it was already too late for the health worker as the police officer who follows the chairman around was sternly given instruction to teach the health worker some lesson for not able to tame his tongue.

'Mr. Chairman, Sir! I am sorry for upsetting you!' he said, bowing down.

The chairman ignored him and walked straight into the house of Mallam Garuba while the police ordered the health worker to follow him to the local police station, where he was detained and locked in jail.

'The chairman has ordered that you spend a while here while you learn some morals on speaking,' said the police man that brought the health worker to the cell.

On the other hand, in Mallam Garuba's compound, the environment which is supposed to be booming with marriage rite activities is drastically turning into a cemetery-like scene as the sudden and strange disappearance of Fatimah remained an obscurity yet to be unveiled and fathomed, even though friends and well-wishers are still trooping in to witness the unfortunate happy event.

'But where could this girl be?' Mr. Garuba again soliloquized. He seems to be more and more confused each moment he tries to find answers to this rhetoric.

The time, being no ones' acquaintance keeps ticking as fast as it should. But to Mr. Garuba, it seems the time has joined force with his daughter to bring him irrefutable shame and disgrace as it seems to him that the clock ticks faster than normal or necessary.

While still battling in his mind to get some answer to his daughters where-about, Fatimah's mother emerged from inside to break the sad the news that their guests were already fuming and almost ready to storm out of their compound if answers are not being provided to their curiosity.

Mallam Garuba hesitantly walked out to meet his supposed-in-laws in the courtyard which now looks much tensed and obviously lean.

'My guests,' he said in a worrisome tone, 'Why do you all seem to be unperturbed by the turn of events? My daughter, who's supposedly your bride has disappeared into thin air within the shortest period and none of you seem to feel concerned not even you the groom,' he pointed his index finger to the sixty-five years old Alhaji Hamza who's supposed to be Fatimah's husband.

Alhaji Hamza stood up in his white regalia, adjusted his already fitted cap sitting on his head and cleared his throat typical of an intro to a wealthy man's speech.

'Well...Sirki... in as much as we are not happy about the way the event turned out, we as well frown at the way you manage your house-hold. What's happening now is a clear indicator that your family is not totally under your subjection as the headman. And I'm sorry, that we cannot be a party to this.' He paused for a while and continued. 'I think the best thing right now is to give you time to figure out and to solve your problems while we await your call.'

The suitors, all looking disappointed, rise and made their way out of Mallam Garuba's compound muttering words that only their ears and hearts could grasp.

The suitors made their way out, followed by friends and well-wishers who all left one after the other. Soon, the compound was left with Mallam Garuba and his immediate family. The house, which was earlier brightened by seemingly happy people has now turned to a mourning domain as everyone goes about with a gloomy face all to the courtesy of Fatimah's whirlwind disappearance. Everyone earnestly wished for a miracle that could give them a clue of Fatimah's whereabouts that alone would at least brighten their hope of getting her back. However, this wish seems to be unfulfilled as the sun set heralds the entry of the night.

———≫•◦•≪———

'Fatimah dear, at this point, what do you intend doing?' Dr. Amina Yaro asked in anticipation.

Fatimah, who's almost recovering from the shock of her parents trying to marry her off at such tender age, also nurses the fear that they would soon trace her to Dr. Amina's abode. At such, it may mean another throng of severe punishment that it would have been far better if she hadn't make the bold attempt to elope in the initial instance, she thought.

'Ma, I just want to leave and never return until my dreams are achieve,' Fatimah replied after minutes of absolute silence to sum up her thoughts and to come up with the conclusion made.

Dr. Amina has secretly nursed the feelings too that soon enough Fatimah's parents may get to know their daughter's hide out, and that may transcend to a whole lot for her taking special cognizant of the fact that the environment is at logger head with her for kicking against child marriage and the sort.

But in as much as she doesn't want to arouse the society rage, she is as well not willing to give Fatimah up to her familiar abductors and abusers who are utmost willing to trade her glaringly beautiful future for anything profitable to them alone not to take to mind her comfort. This situation appears to be as though she is caught up in the circle of the devil and the deep blue sea.

CHAPTER THREE

The long-wait

The ta-ta-ta-ta of the rain drop on pans gradually decreases and the sun is slowly coming out of her tabernacle. Everywhere is refreshing. Leaves on trees dance rhythmically to the song of the breeze. Some birds also hover in the sky, enjoying the restoration of their freedom after the downpour.

Mallam Abdullah Garuba's family seem not to take note of this aesthetic nature. They still grieve the disappearance of their daughter and sibling, Fatima. They have searched the croons and crannies of the village and even some neighbouring villages but all to no avail. It has been an uneasy period of their lives so far. If the search was successful, Mr. Garuba would have gone to Friday Jumat prayers to perform Zakat to show appreciation to the divine. Though Mr. Garuba tried hard to hide his grief because he is the head of the family, anyone who sees him can easily tell that he is not in a good state of mind as a result of the disappearance of the daughter. He couldn't cry out, but his heart was of a surety heavier than a metal stone if weighed under a scale. This was well indicated by his constant reddish eyes developed all of a sudden at the disappearance of Fatimah.

'What doom have I brought upon myself?' he soliloquized. At this point, his mind had drawn a battle line between himself and himself. A part of him almost condemn him to death as to why he never allowed the young teenage girl follow her path of being educated academically, why he didn't give the poor little Fatimah the chance to self-expression. Perhaps this wouldn't have happened. While this condemnation was on in his mind, another part of him raised to counter the first argument; it seems to reassure him that he wasn't wrong by choosing a path for her daughter. 'I am just trying to secure a good future. I am just trying to get her settled maritally which is one of the most important pillars of Islam. I don't think I have done any evil here that will warrant her to make a sudden disappearance of herself leaving everyone in the dark of where she could be found.' This was the war that raised in his mind continually.

For Fatimah's mother, her sorrow seemed to know no end. For in as much as it pained her husband, she is inarguably the worst hit of the incident. For the last five days, she has refuted the objection of consolers to eat any edibles as she sobs bitterly, lying helplessly on the floor, constantly resounding, *'L-ai-la inla-llah...,'* as often as her almost fading strength can carry her. Reminiscing on her last instruction to Fatimah not to go to school that day was a catalyst to her sorrow; she wished she hadn't given that instruction to Fatimah. She wished she had summoned the courage to attack her husband over his decision to give Fatimah out in marriage at a tender age. Even if it would have been a brutal attack, it would have yielded a positive result for not only her daughter but herself. Mama Fatimah really longed and wished she could turn the hands of time to that fateful Monday Fatimah hung her bag heading to school.

'Yah Allah!' she cried out again in agonizing tone. She wailed and rolled on the ground, causing much dust. But she doesn't really care about the dust. If generating much and much of it will bring about her daughter's return, then she doesn't mind doing it over and over again. All she ever needed right now is for her daughter to appear just the exact way she disappeared.

'Mama Fatimah, please take something... even if it's just Kunu Dawa, at least to help you regain some strength,' said one of the women who came to console her.

'Of what use is food to me when my daughter cannot be found. Why should I feed when I'm not certain whether my only daughter has fed or not. Far be it from me to feed when my eyes are yet to see my daughter.' She replied in a wavering weak voice which was accompanied by hot tears ever flowing from her already squinty eyes. Those eyes were obviously almost getting sick of shedding tears but then, they have no choice than to supply when the demand is made.

As it is the right thing typical of the Muslim culture, Mallam Garuba consulted quite a number of his religious superiors (sheikh) to at least reveal the obscurity behind his misery through making *dua* (prayers), but all of them seem to be in one accord in their findings; they all pointed out that Fatimah's disappearance was for a reason, but at the moment, they couldn't pin point the exact reason. They however gave the charge that Mallam Garuba should just continue in prayers for her daughter's safety and wellbeing anywhere she is by waking up in the midnight to make *Nafulath* (mid-night prayers) for her as he anticipates her return.

⟫◦⟪

Saturday morning was a dream come true for Fatimah. Dr. Amina Yaro has made an arrangement for Fatimah's travel from the community to a place where she would be more secured and safe. Dr. Amina Yaro, in the previous week had put a call through to her colleague, Mr. Pwajok in Jos who is also an advocate against girl child marriage.

Mr. Pwajok was Dr. Amina's colleague and classmate abroad where she obtained her degree in law. Seeing that Dr. Amina was the only black woman in their class at that time, he took special interest in her and they became very good friends.

Their friendship continues even at the end of their degree program in school. They became intimate friends who even shared the same ideology about the ill fate of the girl child in the society, especially in the Northern part of Nigeria where they hailed from. They soon begin to work together, advocating for the female child for positive change to manifest in the country. From that time, Mr. Pwajok and Dr. Amina Yaro have been together in the tussle to douse the menace of girl child marriage.

'Fatimah, you will be traveling to Jos this Saturday to go and stay with my friend over there. I am quite optimistic that you will have a better chance to continue your education and fulfil your dream over there than being here with me.' Dr. Amina paused to observe Fatimah's countenance. Being a social psychologist, she could tell that her idea wasn't really going down well with Fatimah, she continued 'Sooner or later, your parents may discover that you took shelter in my home, and you know what that may translate to if I keep on to harbor you. I think traveling out of this state is the best option you can ever leverage on for now if you really wish to make your dreams come true. Don't fret, I promise to give you the best support you'll ever need as a child to actualize your dream. Trust me that you're always in a safe hand even right there in Jos.'

After a long silence, Fatimah finally spoke up with a broad grin. She thanked Dr. Amina for her display of love and care for the period of her stay in her house and as well taking her interest at heart as to send her to a place where she could finally find self-expression and actualization.

To Fatimah, her day of freedom has finally arrived;

she could glaringly see the light at the end of the tunnel and she is fully ready to embrace this light she envisage so that it can shine forth.

While on her bed that night, Fatimah could not stop thinking about her life of freedom that will soon come. Her life becomes real to her than it was from the beginning. She begins to look into the future; she would stand in the front of a crowd of people and tell them about her ordeals in life and how she gained her freedom from the menace of their cultural practice. She could locate her parents among the crowd, all in standing ovation to welcome her home.

Fatimah's thought about her parents drastically reduced the intensity of her elation and as well transported her back to the reality that she may never get to see her parents for a very long if she will ever see them. No doubt, she loves them, but she can't afford to be bought into misery and penury for the rest of her life by those same parents she loves. She had rather draw the margin; she either sacrifice her dreams to gain approval from family while at her own detriment or defy her societal norms infested with misery and shame on the girl child to actualize her dream. *'I have certainly chosen the right path, and that's where I'll thread,'* she finally resolved as she forced herself to sleep.

The rest of the days passed by in peace in Dr. Amina's home. Fatima is also thankful that she is too busy to think about her parents, or even the pathetic look in her mother's eye when her father introduced the old man that was to marry her before she escaped to Dr. Amina's house. In fact, she did not even give another thought of her mother until late that night when Dr. Amina informed her she will be leaving for Jos that night.

'Pwajok. How are doing?' Dr. Amina spoke softly, welcoming Pwajok as he stepped inside. Just then the power supply cut off. This is a usual thing that happens especially in this part of the country. This has made many houses rely on their cheap Chinese generators which always give out smoke and noise. Only the politicians are able to afford heavy duty Japanese or German generators. The poor power situation has been there as long as Dr. Amina can remember, even when she was a kid, nothing has changed. Most people wonder if it is a deliberate act by the politicians and those in authority to impoverish the people. In fact, there are no basic amenities for the people.

'Is the driver taking Fatima to Jos ready to move now?' she asked.

'There is a very serious problem, Amina,' Pwajok replied roughly. The atmosphere became tensed at once. Fatima becomes apprehensive. She moves towards Dr. Amina, her eyes gazing steadily at the doctor. Dr. Amina broke the deafening silence when she noticed that the situation was getting caustic, 'Pwajok, please speak. What is the issue?'

'The po...po...po...liceeeeeee,' he stammered.

'What about the police?' Dr. Amina asked anxiously.

'They are everywhere looking for Fatima, even at the car park. Some even confronted me on the road, threatening that they will close down our NGO. They said that we are going against the culture and tradition of our nation. They accused you in particular of sponsoring rebellion in families.'

'We need to act very fast!' Dr. Amina screamed, looking at Fatima. 'Fatima, go and hide in the bunker, fast! Take everything that could incriminate us. I mean all your things and move into the bunker until the coast is cleared.'

Dr. Amina is a very resolute woman, ever prepared to counter any obstacle that surfaces in her moves. The bunker is a part of her house that nobody can notice except if it is shown. Many young under aged girls have passed through that place to freedom. The local police have ransacked the house severally and are unable to detect the bunker. The compulsory point of call when any child bride is missing is Dr Amina's house. She is secretly admired by young girls who are majorly victims of child marriage but she is severely hated by the local authority who sees her action as profanity and awakening the sleeping resistance among the docile poor because all the victims of child bride are the very poor. The rich sends their daughters to school abroad or private institutions in the country which are preserved for the rich.

Some minutes later, two of the local police matched angrily to Dr. Amina's house with a search warrant, half expecting to find the door locked, but when they knocked and banged the door very recklessly and turned the handle open, the door gave way easily. They walked into the house shouting, 'Where is she? Where is she?'

Dr. Amina and Pwajok stood up against the police men's charge and retorted simultaneously, 'Where is who?' They have been in this game for a long time, they refused to be intimidated by any police. They have been detained severally for this fight against child marriage and they are not about to give up the fight. "We are looking for Fatima, where did you keep her?' retorted, one of the police officers.

Dr Amina feigned surprise, looking at Pwajok, 'Who is Fatima?' Pwajok replied the police men disdainfully, 'Please, Fatima is not here, search for her somewhere else.' The police were very convinced that Fatimah was not there, so they didn't search the house thoroughly. If Fatima was there, the door would not have been left ajar, they thought. More so, there was no way Fatima would be here because Dr. Amina wasn't notify of their coming. The police men left with a conclusion that Fatima has escape from the town and may have run to a relative far away from the village.

One of the police men looked at Dr. Amina for a while and observed her expression. Then he asked in a soft pleading tone, 'Madam we are hungry. Anything for the boys?' Dr. Amina was irritated but she tried to hide her feeling. She put her hand in the bag and gave him two five hundred naira notes, 'Please manage this one.' The police stretched his hand like a hungry beggar and quickly deeps the notes in his pocket. He walked away briskly, pushing his colleague along.

About an hour later, Dr. Amina called Fatima's name thrice before she responded, and Pwajok found this highly amusing. Fatima smiled in good –natured at Pwajok's laughter as she made her way to Dr. Amina. While in her hide out, she was frightened, thinking that the police have discovered her. However, now, her the anxiety is replaced with a smiling demeanor.

'We have to move immediately now that we have diverted the attention of the police,' Dr. Amina said, looking at Fatima.

'I think we need to wait for few more days for the dust to settle,' replied Pwajok.

Dr. Amina shook her head in disapproval, 'WE NEED TO MOVE NOW.'

'If you think so, we need a vehicle that will not raise any suspicion like a good Suv.' Pwajok was still talking when a knock was heard at the door. Quickly, Dr. Amina rushed towards the door to check who was knocking while Fatima ran back to her hide out.

The knock became louder, followed by a shout, 'Open this door now or I break it down!'. Dr. Amina opened the door and saw two men standing outside.

'What do you want?' Queried Amina.

'I am detective Shehu and this is my colleague, detective Umar,' one of the policemen said ceremoniously.

'So what do you want in my house and why were you banging my door like that?" Amina enquired.

'It has been reported at the station that you kidnapped a girl called Fatima,' Shehu retorted.

Amina heard those words clearly, she could almost

see them. They seemed to have floated into her right ear and made exit through her left ear. They were now dancing before her eyes as her temper rises. This type of scenario has occurred severally and she begins to reminisce about the past.

'Two police officers just left here and ransacked the whole house but they didn't find anyone. Please, what did you call her name?'

'Fatima,' Shehu responded, almost trusting Dr. Amina's words. 'Anyway, to be sure you are not hiding the girl in your house, we need to search the house.'

'Where is your search warrant?' Amina asked in confidence.

Umar flashed it on Amina's face.

'Can you lead us into your various rooms?'

'Of course. Let's go. I have no cockroach in my cupboard,' she responded confidently again.

They had barely searched two rooms when they gave up the search noticing the calmed character of Dr. Amina. The two detectives left the house believing Fatima was not there.

After a while, Pwajok walks up to the bunker, 'Hello, Fatima!' He shouted from the entrance of the bunker, tapping the entrance lid. Fatimah looks up from where she is sitting and peeped through the secret inspection hole. This is the safest part of the house. The entrance is flushed with the wall. Fatima opened the door and came out quietly, now unsure of her safety.

'My dear Fatima, we have seen a lot in the last few hours. In this type of situation we receive police men but not at this rate. I am sure more police and detective will still come. Therefore we need to wait for some days before you travel as earlier suggested by Pwajok,' she paused looking into the blank wall, now getting very emotional. "Fatima, we have known each other for just few weeks, and I have loved you every minute. You know, your story is very similar to mine. I ran away from home to pursue my dreams. I was harassed, humiliated, chained until a Good Samaritan helped me. Today, I have a Doctorate degree, Fatima. So do not fear, be strong, okay?' Fatima nodded, totally overwhelmed by Amina's story.

'Fatima, are you alright?'

'Yes, I am.' Fatima answered awkwardly and knelt down to appreciate her for supporting her through all the troubles she has put her through.

"Stand up my dear. We are in this together all the way," she pulled her up and locked her in a warm embrace.

Although Dr. Amina had a restful night, she stayed back home and didn't go to work in the morning. She spent a long time reading from her Koran the fourth chapter of the Quran, surah an-Nisa which addresses the mutual rights of human beings and foundation for a sound family life. After that she goes to take a leisurely bath, washed her hair and allowed it to dry. While she did that, Fatima has dished out some bread and fried egg. After Dr. Amina ate to her satisfaction, she started a letter to the Federal Law Makers responsible for making laws for the country. As she begins to write in her quiet room, she realizes how long it has been since she has been alone and how much she misses the solitude.

Dear Federal Law Makers,

It is with very deep pain I write you this letter and that is why the letter is not characterized with hypocritical nicety and greetings.

I wish to draw your attention to the damage currently done to our girl child under the cover of religion. Most of these girls are taken out of school and forced to marry at a tender age. Child early and forced marriage is an issue that disproportionately affects our girls.

When a girl is married at an infantile stage, her opportunity to learn, grow and realize her full potential becomes a mirage. It is pertinent to state here that child marriage encourages sexual activity among girls who are not yet physically or psychologically prepared to handle childbirth. In view of their young age, complications in pregnancy and child birth is very high.

Very suicidal and unacceptable is the fact that child brides are also more likely in majority of the case to have other pregnancy related injuries such as obstetric fistula, which have devastating long term consequences, in all cases I have witnessed, these girls are left to their fate and abandoned by the men who caused it.

Pregnancy at a young age affects the mother and the child. What I am trying to say here is that a child is giving birth to a child. In most cases we have still births and newborn death, low birth weight, preterm delivery and severe neonatal conditions.

Among many other consequences of child marriage, one of the most worrisome is that the child is broken and destroyed, they risk sexually transmitted diseases like HIV. This is because in most cases these little girls are married off to older men with numerous sex partners.

Time is running out for girls at the risk of child marriage. As I write you this letter, there are over a hundred cases of forced marriage taking place in various communities around us here. We are now faced with the problem of more child brides especially during the Covid-19 with the lock down and rather than these parents thinking how to better their lives, they are busy engaging child marriages.

It is not as if what I am writing is new to most of you because most of you are perpetuators of this dastard act. My emphasis here and the main purpose is to let you know that child marriage is a direct threat to the future of the girl child because it robs them the ability to take hold of their future.

I am requesting a legislation to prohibit child marriage in the country consequent on the above.

Thank you,
Dr. Amina.

She felt drained when she finished the letter and decided to sit under the sun to sun-dry her hair. Her mind stayed on the letter~ she knew the letter will be thrown in the trash bin. The one time she led a demonstration against child marriage to the national assembly, it was a very unpleasant experience. She was leading a group of human right activists to demonstrate against child marriage when a child marriage victim died during child birth. The most annoying thing was that the child bride was few weeks above eleven years. There was national indignation and outcry but Dr. Amina was totally aware of the law-makers nonchalant attitude about child marriage. That day, the police threw tear gas and water canisters on the demonstrators. Many were severely injured including Dr. Amina who broke her ankle. The pain from the injury remains till present. She has been in the barricades, passed through hell and hay fire for this struggle.

Some minutes later, Dr. Amina gave Pwajok her ATM card and told him her withdrawal pin which shows an evidence of trust and told him to withdraw an amount of eighty thousand naira. She smiled and gave Pwajok a nod, "The plan has changed. Fatima will be moving to Kaduna instead of Jos as earlier suggested. There is a family who's ready to accommodate her and sponsor her education for about two years. I believe that will give us enough time to plan for her future."

'Why do we need all this money?' Pwajok queried.

'Because she came here with nothing. We need to buy her some decent clothes and at least reduce the burden on the family that will accommodate her in Kaduna.'

Pwajok moved towards the shelve where Dr. Amina keeps her books, removed a folder containing the lists of their sympathizers in Kaduna, and faced Dr Amina again, 'What is the name of this family?'

'Dr. Adamu Fika,' she replied. Pwajok looked through the list but didn't find the name. He handed it to her. But Amina only collected the folder and dropped it on the table. She began to explain. "There are many people who support our struggle who wish not to be identified." Pwajok was unsatisfied with the response and looked at Dr. Amina sternly, "Can you please describe and explain the career of this Samaritan?" He can remember vividly that he knows one Dr. Adamu in Kaduna. He is an established man with very unpredictable character and rumor has it that he beats and treats his wives so badly.

'This one works for the state government in the ministry of social welfare. He is about six-foot-tall on the big side and keeps a bushy hair,' Amina replied.

'I know him! He is the one! He beats his wives and he is gender insensitive. He has a bad record with his wives, because of his influence in the society most especially his position in the ministry of social welfare, he is able to suppress any case brought against him. I think we should look for some other people to take care of this girl.'

'You are only talking about the bad side,' Amina said, shaking her head in disagreement. 'This man has shown more support to fight against child marriage and rape than any person I know. Pwajok are you aware Dr. Adamu has been responsible for the imprisonment of nearly all the people convicted for rape in Kaduna and her environ? Are you aware how this man contributed his personal resources to challenge that high profile rape case concerning that rich business mogul in Zaria against that poor orange seller that became a national issue? The most interesting thing about Dr. Adamu is that all the daughters are educated and married legally in their adults. So how else do you want him to be gender sensitive?'

Pwajok was not totally convinced. He still has some reservation because Dr. Adamu is a string of contradiction, the same man who supports the girl child emancipation is a wife beater. That major character flaw is unacceptable to Pwajok. As a young man growing up, his father was given to Alcohol and anytime he was drunk, his mother became the victim of abuse. Many times, his mother had been rushed to the hospital after he severely beat her. This has remained indelible in the heart of Pwajok so much that he writes off any man that beats up his wife. For Pwajok, no matter how good a man is, if he raises his hand at his wife, he is nothing but a coward and irresponsible husband and father.

———◆———

It was 6am. The Suv Jeep glided through the bad road which is always contracted to the construction company several times but nothing appears to be done. The constructors believe that if the road is repaired, they will not generate money again from it especially from every new government. The rain, accompanied by thundering sound, poured heavily, 'Please slow down the car,' Dr. Amina said, looking outside the window of the vehicle. Fatima was fast asleep having had a very emotional stressful day the previous night. Now, they are on their way to Kaduna, taking Fatima to a safe haven far from her parents to a foster home where she could achieve her dreams. Just then, the rain stopped suddenly. The only sound is now the breeze rustling the car. Fatima, now awake, joins her two heroes, Amina and Pwajok, to give cognizance to nature; the rustling of the leaves and grasses because of the mighty effect of the breeze, the chirping of birds on trees and in flight, and the tearing apart of the sky constantly as a result of the rain. Fatima's face begins to hot. She wants to apologize for the un-bargained stress and obvious trouble she has caused them and for all the sacrifice they are making to save her from the impending doom of their culture. Her chin comes out with steel determination,

'Dr Amina and Mr. Pwajok, you give me comfort and happiness in the face of tribulation. I cannot thank you enough.' She continues, looking straight at Dr. Amina, 'Look at the risk you are taking for a stranger.' The duo looked at each other and gave Amina a smile. 'Our service is to God and humanity, my dear.' Dr. Amina told her.

The atmosphere became tensed once again. Dr. Amina switched on the radio in the vehicle, music buzzes from the local radio station but it was soon interrupted by a public service announcement of a missing girl. The news says that anybody with vital information relating to her where-about should contact the nearest police station. The occupants of the vehicle looked at one another with trepidation. This time accompanied with a silence more dreaded than the previous, owing to the fact that the very missing victim being announced in the community radio is live there with them, hale and seemingly hearty. 'What are we going to do now? The news is already a public concern,' Dr. Amina asked in a less firm voice full of worry and somewhat pessimism.

Mr. Pwajok smiled chiefly and replied 'Common… this isn't the first time a case like this would be reported in either a radio station or television where the pictorial image of the victim would even be displayed and yet nothing fruitful will result from it. So please don't fret about anything because it's not as if we're doing this with any obnoxious intention. It's all for the good of our ward and we are also trying to bring into subjection and perhaps total extinction of some wrong societal ills, you know.' He paused before he continues again, 'Moreover, we are both aware of the society we are. Things like this doesn't take long for it to clear off the air. You know the police are just trying to put a camouflaged action by reporting it on air. Soon enough, everything will be off the air. So please stay put and show no fret,' he concluded with a broad smile as he took a glaring look at Fatimah who's twice as tensed as Dr. Amina.

The announcement went on for three times. No doubt, the sponsors had paid for three slots only in the radio station. The radio resumed its playlist again as it continued with the background music earlier being played, which serve as shield for the subtle silence that has again taken its place in the vehicle as it tries to navigate its way through the pathetically tough road causing the occupants in the vehicle to shoulder-hit one another as the vehicle ride through the unavoidable potholes that characterizes a poorly dejected road which cries profusely seeking urgent attention from anyone ready to help.

<hr />

It's now 10:30 in the evening. Fatima and her heroes have finally arrived their destination, Kaduna state. However, even though the state has it slogan to be the

Centre of learning, nothing seems to be a practical evidence of this assertion. One would have thought that a state with such an enlightening slogan ought to be the envy and a roadmap for some other states in terms of learning new ways of good life such as good roads, steady light and a working infrastructure. But it's quite disappointing that the slogan tends to contradict the reality of Kaduna state. From the outlook and layout of the state, one can swiftly conclude that some archaic ways of living still hold sway in most parts if not in general. The interesting thing however for the three of them is that Fatimah has arrived her pre-supposed safe habitation for better life. And that alone lightened her up as they drive off to Dr. Adamu's resident their host.

Dr. Adamu is an inspector-general of the armed forces in Kaduna who also doubled as an advocate for girl-child marriage in the state. For a man of his status, he lived in the metropolitan part of the state. His hall of residence is located around Tafawa Balewa Road. The street falls among the few privileged ones who are privileged to have a fairly accessible roads courtesy of the fact that some well-meaning individuals have their abodes erected there. However, poor power supply seems to be an epidemic ravaging the entire state as only the ones with the supply of either a power plant or a generator can conquer. This is evident by the mechanized sounds of various power generator being put on by their owners.

Dr. Adamu's residence was part of those houses that sponsors the generator sound.

The vehicle halted as it entered through the open gate of Dr. Adamu's, having honk one to two times alerting the gateman of their arrival and to open up. However, this was not without some interrogation from the gateman seeking to know who and what they want.

The trio alighted, all looking tired and weary. One can tell by the expression on their faces that their journey was nothing short of a stressful one. Fatimah seems to be the worst hit of this stress. This is perhaps her first time she's made such journey; hence the travel fever tends to be more pronounced on her face.

'Asalamu Alekum,' Dr. Amina saluted Dr. Adamu who also replied 'Aleikum Salam,' with a half-smile that revealed some parts of his incisor dentition.

Mr. Pwajok, who stood partly behind Dr. Amina also greeted him with a handshake. As the Islamic law has it, only males are permitted to shake another male. Such is not allowed with male and female as it is seen to be a taboo against the Sharia law.

'Please let's go inside. It is already late.'

Dr. Adamu leads them inside.

Dr. Adamu, being a husband of two wives and father of six children had built his house in a way that is in consonance with his religious belief. His humble edify is a three-bedroom apartment separated by a corridor that distinguishes the males' from the females' apartments. And the law is that no male must encroach the boundary of passing over to the females' apartment except with an order to do that. All females must always be on their hijab in the day time whether inside or outside.

Although he's civilized, his civilization seems not to gain any penetration on his religious and traditional belief. Hence, his household is conducted base on his beliefs.

Dr. Adamu's sitting room is nothing different from a typical northern African man. The cushion looks a bit outdated but still retain its ability to carry the weight of its sitters. A glass round table is placed at the center of the sitting room with a flower vase on its top. Looking at the wall is a gigantic pictorial image of prophet Mohammed hanged at the top side of the wall visible enough to every sight.

Other than these, there's not much of interior decoration that reflect the house extremely fashionable and envied or portray Dr. Adamu as a man with so much feats. Simplicity is the order of custom in his household.

⟫◦⟪

Days gradually turn into weeks, and weeks into months. It's now seven months since Fatimah arrived Dr. Adamu's house in Kaduna. The last six seven months have been terrible. Adamu is away to Europe for a one year course spending only half of the duration and leaving the household under the care of his brother. The acacias had bloomed; the purple ice plants flowered beside the perimeter fence, the mango trees bared fruit but everyone in the household of Adamu were all looking miserable.

The Adamu's house hold is now in turmoil. Adamu's brother who is now in charge of the house, is an irresponsible man and everybody knew the role of caretaker of the house do not suit him, hence people wonder why Adamu left the house under his care. He hardly possessed any positive attribute. His public appearance is characterized by an intense nervy repulsion. He stridently denounced what Adamu stands for as hokum, designed to stifle dissent. At home, his mood was more vexatious. He worried out loud about the near independence the females in the house enjoy, wondering why they must graduate from the university before marriage. Knowing his brother's antecedent, he knew Fatimah was a fugitive running from tradition. He is depressed by what his brother embraces and allows in his house. To him, it's such a vagabond.

Adamu's brother makes life hell for Fatimah as Dr. Adamu's wives watched helplessly. He started making enquiry about Fatima's family background with the sole aim of sending her back to her family. This scheme was revealed to Fatima by one of the wives. She would rather die than to go back to Kano and get married, she thought.

Five days after the secret was leaked to her, Fatimah, after the first cock crowed left the house secretly through the back gate. Fearfully, she entered the city and hurried towards the slum of Kaduna. By the time she got there the day was fully dawn and everywhere was lighted up. This was not her first time of coming here as on several occasion, has been sent on errands but the fear that grips her mind is as a result of the fact that she is now homeless. This time around, she needs a temporary shelter. Luckily, in few minutes, she got a place fifteen minutes work from the place she used to go for errands. Home for Fatimah is worse than opprobrium. The squalid structure built with rotten plywood and covered with torn nylon sheets, nothing protecting her from the elements and vicissitudes of life. The dirty and wet environments is a fertile ground for mosquitoes and rodents.

Weakened by lack of good food and barely eating to survive as one good meal a day is luxury, Fatima's story is that of absolute abandonment, pain and penury. A total display of nefarious, truculent societal lifestyle where the rich oppress the poor. Many People, especially her teachers, may find it difficult to believe that this little girl who has a promising potential is passing through a messy life. Fatimah by nature *never throw in the towel* in the battle to be who she wants to be in life. Many times, she sees the light of many ladies dimed by unexplainable tradition and culture, as *a triton among minnows*, she resolutely and vehemently shows her disdain. She wonders where she got the courage to have left her mother. Most ladies are trained to be timid and subservient even in the case of abuse and disrespect. The fear of being relegated to the dustbin of life makes her even as young as she is, *to put her shoulder to the wheel.*

The odor inside the vicinity of Fatimah's shelter was overbearing. It is dark inside and therefore it takes her some time to recognize people. There are many homeless people like her living there; many of them far older and some much younger especially the young kids between the age of three and ten. This is ridiculously true. The kids move in groups begging for food and at night, they are at the mercy of the elements. Many of them sleep on bare floors and even on heap of dungs. Moving rudderless scavenging for any semblance of edibles.

Fatimah found Musa, a load lifter and driver, on the loading dock at the back of a trailer, preparing to leave that night for Lagos.

'Musa,' Fatimah's voice was urgent. 'I need to talk with you.'

'Wettin be the matter?'

'I want you to help me talk to the driver to take me to Lagos.'

Musa eyed her with a curious look, 'What are you going to Lagos to do? Who do you know in Lagos? Have you been to Lagos before or you want to go and die?'

'I want to go and look for work. Fatimah thrust a paper to him where advertisement for house helps was published. She waited as Musa took the paper to read. She watched the emotions play across his face as he tossed the paper upside down, forgetting that Musa could not read a word in English. Musa returned the paper to Fatimah pretending to have read the content but went further to ask,

'Na wettin the paper dey say?'

Fatimah replied, 'They are looking for house helps in Lagos.'

'Okay. I go look for a good driver wey go take you go Lagos. This one driver I no trust him at all, you hear me so?' he told Fatima who nodded and gave a wry smile.

Musa left home at the age of three as an Almajiri.

CHAPTER FOUR

The Almajiris: anger and hunger

The Almajiri system which is very prevalent in northern Nigeria is supposed to be a system where children are taken to Islamic scholars to educate the children on Islamic education but the current system in Nigeria is a case of wicked abandonment of children to roam the streets with plate begging for food. Many schools of thought believe that the present system is a calculated strategy by the northern elites to create a large pool of innocent ignorant population to be manipulated for election purposes. The Almajiri children are born to suffer. In the park where Musa has been doing a type of menial jobs are many other children with sordid tales that can bring tears to even the hardest men.

The poverty one sees daily in Nigeria and especially in Northern Nigeria is by design and not by accident. Poverty and ignorance are important ingredient for the agenda. The poorer one is, the less one is going to question those who misrule one. This is the fundamental reason for the Almajiri system.

Haruna, an eight year old child with no parents hails from Challawa in Kano state. His teeth and tongue battle each other as he tells his bitter ordeal in his short spam of existence. Although his belief is that his state of life is the will of God for him but the question he is yet to resolve is. *Why are many children not like him who begs and eats from the garbage? Why are some children who are of his age in school and enjoy parental care?*

Haruna explains, 'I don't know where I am from. One man brought me here to be an Almajiri,' he says wiping off the mucus from his nose and with the plate stretched out waiting for little stipends.

Ibrahim, another Almajiri, is a nine year old boy from Yobe state. The weather has not been very friendly these days. The rain pours frequently. Even now, it just stopped raining. In a motor pack in Kaduna, Ibrahim stands beside the driver of the truck, Musa, who is off-loading. He shivers like a wet bird, crying terribly and begs Musa for some food, 'May ALLAH bless you. Please give me food. I have not eaten since morning. Yesterday night, I slept with an empty stomach. Please for Allah sake,' he chants in a typical Hausa language.

The rhythm of his chant reveals that it is a constant thing in his life. He holds his big bowl firmly. Musa, who is already irritated by the delay in loading of his vehicle, and is not in the mood for such generosity, retorted, 'Why your Alfa not give you food that you say you have not eat since morning?'

An Alfa is the clerical guardian who caters for the living of abandoned children and orphans given to his custody. However, this is always the other way round in most northern parts of the country. Instead of caring for the children, he buys plates and places them in their hands for the begging of food and alms collection. Ibrahim walked quietly away from Musa to another person for alms.

The heart breaking situation of Ibrahim is traditionally the way of life of countless number of northern forgotten children only remembered for political purposes such as campaign and other political manipulations. Millions of out of school children roam the major city streets all over northern Nigeria with big bowl in their hands.

They are born to suffer the vicissitude of life. They mostly take to begging as a carrier from up till age seventeen. By this time they are used to all kinds of drugs like tramadol and codeine. The children soon grow to become delinquent and also engage in odds job in the day and robbery at night waiting for the whistle to unleash the mayhem and terror of any perceived enemy of the elites who put them in this sorry state. They are best described as inmates of the streets, instruments in the hand of the soulless elites and fragments of the wretched poor.

On daily basis, the streets in major cities in northern Nigeria are clogged with Almajiri. They are given specific instruction by their clerical guardians to go begging for alms and hassle for food after reading their Quranic symphonies every morning. This happens from daybreak to nightfall. These children become subjected to every imaginable hazard on the street in the course of pursuing their daily meal. They perch like bees on windows of eateries. As soon as a customer gets up to ease himself or to get something, the kids attack the food on the plate with viciousness not minding weather the customer will come back to his food or not. How will these forgotten children survive if they don't beg or hassle for food? This the question the elites never ask or care to answer. The very painful thing is that the agony and pain these minors are made to go through is direct opposite of the character of the creator being taught the kids. They see it is a contradiction being told the creator is most merciful and most beneficial and yet their lives is the opposite of mercy and benefits, no wonder as they get older to resort to drugs and crime.

Not very far from where the truck going to Lagos is being off-loaded were another group of Almajiri. Their ambience dispatches what can best be described as 'orphans of living parents'.

Handsome, slim and tall for his age, is Tambuwa who speaks timidly with funereal tone. As he speaks, tears flows freely from his eyes. He stands at a vintage point, seeking money or food from people, rather than giving him some alms, many people spend time appreciating his beauty and leave him hungry. 'I have never seen my parents. Somebody brought me here for Arabic school some years ago and since I came here, the person never comes back. I was little when I was brought here. I don't know where I am brought from too.'

Tambuwa does not also know his exact age, but he should be between eight and ten years old. As young as he is, he has been toughened by the vicissitude of life. He labours like an elephant but eats like an ant under the scourging sun every day. This explains the frequent free flow of tears in his tender face. Most of the times, he serves as an errand boy and carries goods on his head and in return the customers give him tokens at their discretion.

'Whenever we finish the morning Qur'anic lessons, I come here to look for food. Sometimes I am lucky. I meet good people. And sometimes I meet wicked people who do not even give me anything in return. Whenever I have no meagre work to do, I resort to begging of alms. Many times, however, I sleep with empty stomach.' Next to Tambuwa is Lamido, who is one or two years younger than Tambuwa. Lamido, like Tambuwa, has no proper care from his Alfa and has no permanent shelter. He could sleep in the thatch or in a corner of the road very late in the night. Lamido has survival instinct. When he is hungry, he tries to snatch ones food but if one refuses to give it to him, he forcefully takes it from one. And how humongous his strength at a very young age! He hardly knows the difference between right and wrong. He is from Jigawa state. Initially, his journey to Kaduna was to acquire his preliminary Islamic studies. Sadly, his father who had brought him three years ago never looks back at his son. The father has over seventeen children from four wives and he still wants more. Tired of this disjointed impoverished childhood, Lamido had tried to run away from his Islamic guardian who would only ask him to beg and beg and expect a return from him and other Almajiris under his custody. Lamido sadly tells his co-Almajiris that he is still under the subjection of their Alfa because he has nowhere to run to. He envies other privileged children of his age who go to school, especially those whose parents employ some chauffeurs to drive them to school driven. He has severally asked his Islamic teacher why God makes some people like him to be born to suffer while others are enjoying but the teacher did not answer the question, he only shouted at him and thrust a plate which was broken at the edge at him. As Lamido tried to pick it, the teacher drew the plate back with force which led to his index finger being injured with profuse bleeding. He could not fathom the level of cruelty coming from such a religious leader.

Lamido was lost in thought with fixed gaze at a young boy of his age sitting in a jeep with a police escort waiting for the mother who alighted from the car to buy some fruits. Just then he breaks the few minutes silence and tries to draw the emotional attention of passerby to his reddened eyes, 'Look at me, I have been begging since morning and nobody has given me anything. No food, no money. But you look at that boy sitting inside a big car guarded by a police man. What crime have I committed to come to this life? Who have I offended? Why is life treating me like this?'

As Lamido was still complaining out loud, a group of young boys between the ages of seven and eight years swarmed round the jeep. The police man shouted at them, 'Leave this place!' But the boys refused to go and even more boys started coming to the scene with plates in their hands. By this time they have surrounded the vehicle stretching out their plates. These ones will not talk or move unless you buy them food or give them money. Most of them found themselves in such situation because they are banished from their home and told never to come back again. These children are deadened to feelings and repercussion, going through sharp attack of mental anguish, their travails as children and human beings born by a man and woman but parented by nobody. Most of these children have not only forgotten their homes but their homes have totally forsaken them and do not desire their return because they consider the purpose of their birth was strictly for population dominance. Many have wondered the purpose of giving birth to children and throwing them to the streets with plates in their hands begging for survival have turned many of them to beast. They are become primitive and unreasonable. They have been dejected and rejected from their homes which most of them never even know their origin because they have been abandoned and rejected right from childhood. They are unlearned children. They wander the streets with torn clothes. They are not also given proper health care in their community as it is given other children with well to do parents. They get nothing from society but scorn and rejection yet their number increases day by day.

However on that day, the boys were lucky the madam that brought the parked vehicle shared some money to all of them. She knew that was the only way the vehicle could leave that place unscratched.

The swarm of children moved to a nearby restaurant. It was a day of ill-luck for most of the hungry and permanently angry abandoned children of the street. The scavenging children stood at the entrance of the restaurant vigilantly peeping into the restaurant for leftovers to fight over. The owner of the restaurant, a dismissed police officer, seriously irritated by their presence. The dismissed police officer could no longer stomach their presence. He carried a stick, telling them to 'Go away from here, wretched things.' 'These scavengers are embarrassing my customers and are messing up this place,' he frowns, shouting at the top of his voice, and waving the stick at them. When they refused to move, he splashed dirty water on them.

Buhari stands a bit aloof watching a customer through the window. His eyes counted each spoon of rice the customer put in his mouth. He had hardly stood up to get serviette from two tables away, that, like a thunder bolt, Buhari jumped through the window and emptied the whole plate in his mouth in two strikes. This action irked the dismissed police officer and he hit Buhari with the stick he was holding but that did not stop him from still leaking the plate with his tongue. After he did enough justice to the plate, he muttered, "We come here every day to beg for what to eat. All you do is to insult us as if we were the ones that put ourselves in this condition.' The customer whom Buhari ate his food was bemused but other customers present were not surprised because it is a common occurrence here. It is advisable that if one is eating, one should not get up till one finishes eating if not these angry children would not only consume ones food but also the plate. The customer who now got furious, laments, 'These children don't even have morals.' 'It is highly irresponsible to abandon children like this, anyway. The annoying thing is that these men are still busy impregnating underage girls!" Another customer commented bitterly.

The dismissed police officer who runs the restaurant tried to pacify the customers,

'Even if you send them away, they will not go. They don't care because they are not trained. They are loosed canon but guarded missiles waiting for elections and riots. You see, that is why I call them guarded missiles.'

Another customer who tries to be mild in his assertion says, 'Although the begging propensities of these children is very annoying and totally unacceptable, but as a pure Muslim I will not criticize them because they serve our advantage. What they came to do is good because they seek knowledge. But our leaders never help them so they have no other way but to beg.'

The dismissed police officer was still very vexed that the boys have not left. This time he began to shove and push them out of the restaurant. A customer left his seat and grabbed the dismissed police officer by the hand and started shouting at him,

'Even though they are in your restaurant, you have no right to bully them. There is no alternative for these children, I expect you to know that. It is no fault of the innocent children but their misguided parents,' he paused, then continues advocating for the children, 'In Nigeria, especially in the north, the rights of the children are brazenly trampled upon without fear of the law. What am I even saying? Which law, sef? There is no law that cautions the irresponsible attitudes of the parents towards their children! The child rights act has been deliberately frustrated from taking its root. If the law was embraced, parents in question would have been held responsible for this mindlessness.'

While the Almajiri children were still there with their plates waiting for money and food, one of the prominent politicians walked into the vicinity. Many people started chanting his praise and he waved his hand randomly and threw money to the air. There was a mad rush. Everywhere was upside down. The Almajiri children overturned everywhere picking crisps of money falling to the ground. People call this politician king of the dead, though no one ever said it to his face. His real name is Alhaji Buka. Sometimes when he hears the nick name, he smiles to himself. His major aim is traversing the land to seek for political support. Sometimes he detects a note of sarcasm of words like *thief returning small portion of the loot* when he throws money around. Sometimes the whispers held a tremolo of disquiet, like the murmurs of the purely religious person as a dubious stranger passes among them. It was unbelievable to those who could not understand while he keeps winning election despite the fact that almost everybody, apart from the Almajiri children, knows him as merchant of death. He is one of those promoting the Almajiri system because he leverages on the ignorance of the people and the system. Does he enjoy the continual destruction and impoverishment of his people, they wonder? Does the condition of these little children whose future are virtually destroyed hold such an allure for him that he has turned his back on doing the right thing? They think this cannot be normal and they cast uneasy glances his way noticing details that confirms his heartlessness by his cynical mocking facial looks when he throws money at the down trodden. His flamboyant life styles, moving in convoy of expensive vehicles, over flowing clothes, wristwatch costing millions of dollar, and most of all the way he throws the money about disturbs the discerning but Almajiri, who to them is their hero. Anybody that gives them stipends is a hero. The dismissed police officer walked up to him and confronted him,

'Alhaji, why are you deceiving these people like this?'

The politician marveled at the effrontery of the owner of the restaurant, looking furious, he said,

'How dare you question my actions? Do you want to die? You dismissed criminal police officer. If you don't leave here now I will make your life miserable.'

The dismissed police officer hissed, and replied out loud,

'My life cannot be more miserable than what you have done to these children!'

Infuriated, the politician instructed his thugs to beat him up. All entreaties from the customers were rebuffed. He needed to use the dismissed police officer as an example for others to learn how the politicians run things here: our pocket first. Nothing else matters. This explains the perennial underdevelopment and backwardness lack of hospital and other basic necessities of life. The level of poverty gets higher every day but the politicians care less about the populace and continue to live a flamboyant life, even buying properties from Europe and America.

Later, the politician grabbed the handle of the car and jumped into the car, shouting at the top of his voice, 'increase the air conditional,' he was swimming in a sea of humidity. Oddly, he was sweating in the late afternoon heat. He looked outside the window of the car and said out loud, 'The sun is going down.' The car set off immediately down the road amidst cheers from the wretched and conquered. Tall grass obscured the path, and blocked drains with dirt everywhere, the average politician here does not give a damn.

The dismissed police officer and one of his customers who emerged from the scene the politician just exited brazenly, and stepping over the drainage which by now is filled with dirt and stagnant water, shook their heads in disdain.

The hot wind flapped their coats and whipped their faces as they headed into the restaurant where new set of Almajiri boys have just come to scavenge for leftover food. Their eyes narrowed against the young unkempt dirty looking sets of boys. As they stepped into the restaurant, the dismissed police officer registered a whisper of despondency against the presence of the boys. He smelled something like spoilt broken eggs and a mixture of old paint. He waved towards the young boys, and signaling them to move away to a safe distance to reduce the smell of their filth. The clatter of chinaware attracted the dismissed police officer down the inner corridor to the kitchen awash in fluorescent light, a disconcerting modern detail. It glared down and unflattering, on the deeply lined faces of the cooks sweating profusely and stirring different pots of soup and foods on top of fire place. Their sweat falling freely on the food. There were just six of them. Their attention was focused on getting the food ready because the customers were getting inpatient. The dismissed police office watched as arthritic hands of one of the cooks scooped the bowl of mixed flour into the serving tray without any consideration for hygiene. Another cook sat slumped in a swivel chair. She tilted to a corner and helped herself with a big bone of meat in her mouth. She was the first to notice their boss, the dismissed police officer, coming. When she signaled to the other cooks their boss's arrival, they quickly adjusted and cleaned up their mess. Many of them wiped their sweat with the back of their aprons trying to look very neat and clean before their boss.

Gazing into those frightened faces, the dismissed police officer was startled by the frailty combined with the untidiness he saw. They are cooks who do not show happiness or pleasure in doing their job. The dismissed police officer always sees in their faces bewilderment and questions of why they are made to pass through the tragedy of being locked in an oven with peanuts as pay, and apart from left overs, there has never been food for them, the cooks. To make matters worse for the cooks, before they lay claim to the left over foods, the Almajiri would have grabbed and started feasting on them.

The dismissed police officer met one of the cooks who just came in from the back of the kitchen where she went to collect some fire wood, and asked her angrily, 'Can you tell me why this place is so unkempt and why you are pouring your sweat into the food you are coking?'

The question was answered by this harried looking cook who is tired of the whole job and the poor condition they are subjected to. She was dressed in a faded red jumper stitched at different places and stained with oil. Ants were running out of the wood she was carrying and some happily dropped into the pot on the fire. It is obvious she is not a trained cook and an unhappy one too. She has only succumbed to this job because of her family hardship and her husband joblessness.

'You are talking of unkempt place when you don't care about our welfare. Are we responsible for the sweat when you have refused to provide adequate ventilation,' the woman responded ready for any confrontation and consequences.

He looked at her with disdain and cocked his head towards the doorway. The boss's strand of dyed hair fell off into the pot of food as a result of a sudden rush of breeze from the entrance at the back. He walked away from the kitchen to the eating room.

Meanwhile, before the dismissed police officer could get back to the main restaurant, more of the Almajiri children were there hitting their plastic plates meant for begging food and money in rhythmic synchronized and melodious manner. The dismissed police officer was overwhelmed as he graciously looked at them. Something he had never heard thought before. *Damn… These boys are creative*, he thought. "I think, if you boys are going to be coming here to scavenge for left overs you must be making this sonorous music to entertain the guest" he joked. He knows actually that no amount of music can replace their nuisance value. He doled out money to each of them telling them to leave the place politely. The kids thanked him in awe, finding it hard to believe how generous he suddenly became and not sure if it was the rhythm they were dishing out or if God suddenly touched his heart. After giving them the money, he told them to always come after closing of the restaurant so that they could share the leftover food with those who came to pick the same leftover food for their dogs and other animals.

CHAPTER FIVE

Frying pan to fire

Musa kept to his word to help Fatimah get a good driver that will take her to Lagos. He negotiated with a driver going to Lagos to pick Fatimah at no cost on the condition she will seat on the attachment. The attachment is a small stool placed in the back part of the aisle. Each time any of the people with legitimate seat wants to alight for any reason, people sitting in the attachment must step aside squeezing their body to a side seat. This makes the attachment seat extremely uncomfortable. Fatima's intention was to go to Lagos and work for some time before she goes back to school to complete her education. It has remained her burning desire to get good education and come back to the north to fight against child marriage. This has been her dream before she found herself as a victim such that is even fighting for her survival now.

Fatimah arrived the motor park many hours before the departure time to avoid missing the vehicle because Musa had told her how difficult it was to get a good driver like this one who is sympathetic and empathetic and will surely treat her like his daughter. Fatimah stood beside the long luxurious clean bus which will soon be heading for Lagos in the next two hours. She stared at herself in the mirror and didn't like what she saw. She compares herself to her mentor, Dr. Amina Yaro, the crusader against child marriage, who always look regally serene and in control, always well kept. She wears a glossy slash lipstick of red on a flawless skin. Most young girls look up to her. The image Fatimah saw in the mirror is neither serene nor flawless. Her hair is wild like an overgrown bush~ the black coils revealing a pale and strained face. *I am not myself,* she thought. *'I can't recognize this person in the mirror. What happened to me?'* she queried herself.

Suddenly she felt like nauseating. She closed her eyes, tightened her fist, trying to fight it. Her trip can be aborted if the driver thinks she is sick. Unfortunately for her, sheer will power couldn't hold back the inevitable but was able to delay the time of release. Clapping her hand in her mouth, she dashed to the back of the park where refuse is dumped, getting there just in time. Even after her stomach has emptied itself, she lingered there with her hand hung over the wall of the dumpsite waiting for the pain on her abdomen to subside. She didn't panic because she knew that she will be relieve after the vomit.it is a symptom of her menstrual flow. She is happy this happened before the bus gets filled with passenger. It would have been a huge embarrassment and inconvenience for her and the other passengers if she had emptied her stomach in the bus. Few minutes later, Fatima straightened and stepped out of the dump site. She moved to a nearby running water, washed her face, scooped water into her mouth to rinse it off the sour taste, and splashed more water on her face. She tied a flowery scarf on her hair and suddenly looks different from the same person she saw on the mirror few hours ago. She felt relieved and her stomach settled. Fatima braced herself up, "Stand up girl and don't be defeated! You have gone too far to surrender. Lagos await for you!" When all the trace of the nausea has disappeared, she felt so drained and sat down on a wooden bench waiting for the time the vehicle will be ready for boarding. She thought about the work that awaits her in Lagos and the frustration of the hectic life in Lagos where everything is on high speed compared to the north where things are a bit slow and normal. She remembered how she tried to hide useful information about her trip to Lagos from Musa because she thinks he has a narrow mind being an Almajiri before he became a loader in motor packs. He has never been to Lagos and he does not want Fatimah to get the faintest idea he does not know Lagos.

She became tired of sitting and waiting for passengers to fill the bus. Some passengers have started coming and taking their time to pay for the transport and in turn get their tickets. Usually those with money to buy the ticket don't come to the park to wait unnecessary. They come few minutes to the departure of the bus. She feels reluctant to step away from the park to a proper place where she would have some rest before the stressful journey begins, where no one could glimpse the turmoil written on her face. She wonders how the driver will be of assistance to her because the direction of the place she is going to in Lagos is from an old newspaper and she wonders if the advertisement for a house help is still valid. However, her consolation is *Lagos is a big city.* When things don't go well as expected, she will resort to sleeping under the bridge. The time has finally come to board the bus to Lagos. This is the beginning of a new phase of life. If it will be glory or more tears time will tell. Lagos is the place where magic happens; the good, and the bad, and the ugly and the beautiful. The thought fell quietly into place, like a photographer's backdrop unfurling behind the subject of the portrait. Fatimah rushes to enter the bus and in trying to do so caught the attention of the driver, the person expected to guide her to her destination in Lagos. It is how one person and a handful of stories can alter life like this and she still persist despite her age. Eventually Fatimah shuffled in the door and braced her hand on the side chair next to her before taking her seat, her gaze scarfing the bus with the discernment of a leathery old goat sniffing for something to nibble on. Her survey paused momentarily on a pile of aging seat covers heaped on the luggage carriers and took her place on a stool in the walkway of the luxurious bus and leaned her head on the side chair. The routine checks was carried out speedily and it was time for the bus to move. The bus moved and has barely travelled for one hour when a loud sound was heard by the road side. The driver is not unfamiliar with what will happen next. Gun shuts rented the air trying to hit the body of the bus. Shouts and scream also rented the air as the driver tried to escape the ambush. He is such an experienced driver who is ever prepared for any eventuality. The vehicle continues to move in a sinusoidal and swerving manner. The bullet raining from outside constantly hit the bus windows. This time the shouts from the bus have ceased and the sudden silence of the passengers seem even louder than the previous roars and screams. Every eye was riveted on the ground. The hush will only last a while until the blast of a very loud gun hits the back windscreen shattering it into pieces. Not minding the damage, the driver sped on the more. Fatimah fought to shut out the noise and keep her mind wholly centered on getting to Lagos in one piece, but it was impossible. Her brain was bridled with unbidden thought, although what is happening right now is a small thing compared to the vicissitude and travel life has meted her young age. She has lived this terror for all her life as long as she remembers. The fact that the aggressors are still firing at the bus terrified her the more especially since she has been told of how merciless the night robbers are to young women. She has been told of heinous experiences of rape and assault.

She watched as the other passengers cry with agony, contorting their faces. Some of their mouth wide open, gasping of air. The lady sitting on the seat next to her stool had her eyes dropped to the feet of the seat, her teeth gripping the leather and tearing it apart. But even as she watched, her mind remained a jumble of conflicting thought. Suddenly, the gunshots stopped but the bus moves on, swerving as if it was going to fall. It is obvious that the bus has lost balance but the driver continues to speed on. After some time, their pursuers lost them while they moved on to safety.

This type of scenario is a common occurrence on this route and nothing has been done by the police to arrest the situation. It a situation of nobody cares because the night bus movement is meant for the poor. Anything that does not affect the rich is treated with nonchalant attitude. When the aviation workers threatened to go on strike, the government quickly resolved and addressed their concern because the top government officials should be safe while travelling by road. Now apart from the bad roads which are infested with potholes and broken patches, you have the most dreaded fear of kidnappers. These kidnappers are mainly the Almajiri children who have grown beyond mere begging for alms to survive. Hardly does a day pass without a case of people being kidnapped on bad spots of the road. The government officials who manage to go by road are escorted by heavily armed police officials. In some cases the kidnappers attack the convoy, the police men are killed and they make away with their victims. The journey that will take an average of three hours takes about twelve hours as a result of the bad road. Travelling by road in this clime is hellish.

The driver continues to maneuver the bus until it

gets to a check point where police are gathered and stops. The driver fumbles for the door and looks at his watch lying on the floor near the exit door. The time says 3a.m. He is a bit dizzy. He opens the door and tells everybody to get down from the vehicle. They are in a safe place now although they have not covered half of their journey. All the passengers disembarked and the police started interrogating everybody, 'Does anyone of you know any of the robbers?' 'How many are they?' 'What type of car did they drive?' These irrelevant questions continued and the passengers became pissed off. Some of the passengers join the driver to fix the vehicle and replace the flat tyre.

Dawn was just breaking in the Eastern part when the driver finally fixed the vehicle and ordered the passengers to get into the vehicle but the police insisted they pay them for the protection. Grudgingly the driver parted away with some money and the bus commenced its journey to Lagos.

They arrive Lagos in the late afternoon to the welcome of fierce looking and starved area boys.

Fatimah is not unfamiliar with the story of louts, popularly called *area boys*, and other street urchins in Lagos. This is one of the most pathetic situation in a country like Nigeria with all their natural resources not properly harnessed to give the citizens the basic necessities of life. The area boys are a group of homeless children abandoned by their families, sentenced to a regrettable life by the vicissitude of life. They sleep under the bridges and they are very dangerous to passerby. Most of them are drug addicts necessitated by neglect and abandonment. Area boys are dreaded and are believed to be afflicted with timorous vituperation. A visitor's worst nightmare is an encounter with area boys. They don't back down until they get what they are gunning for.

The bus carrying Fatimah eventually entered the park. If a passenger is dropped outside the park, the area boys would lay hold of the driver who would then have to pay through his nose. As the passengers were coming down from the bus, the expected happened. It was like a theater of the absurd, the shouts were deafening. A couple of weird looking boys pounced on an elderly man in the park. As the beating continued with on lookers watching the shout of "Ole, Ole!" Ole is a Yoruba word for thief. What a display of barbarism in the twenty-first century. The victim, an elderly man, has been in that park for many years collecting tolls from the bus drivers. Today, he was paid a toll by the bus driver and quickly hid the money under his pants and grabbed the motor boy claiming that he had not paid. An argument ensued and other area boys came to the scene to apply the normal jungle justice and the money was found under his pants when the elderly man was searched. The elderly man has been getting away with this type of attitude for a long time and many innocent drivers are made to pay twice their tolls.

'Poor man! That is ludicrous,' a Reverend father exclaimed in heavily accented English. He recalled a similar incident he once experienced. A woman was being beaten in similar circumstance and as he tried to intervene to rescue the woman, the fierce looking hoodlums turned the heat on him. Luckily for him, at that time, one of his parishioners who was a military personnel intervened to ward off the hoodlums better described as area boys. Everybody fears the area boys even local government officials who are supposed to control the parks and the police who are supposed to make peace rein in the environment. The passengers at times lose their money to the area boys and there is nobody to help them. 'The attitude of the area boys is not good for business,' the Reverend Father concluded.

Area boys are virtually everywhere in Lagos. You can find them at the motor parks, under the bridges, main roads, markets and everywhere they choose to go. They operate without rules. Area boys are illegal toll collectors powered by the degree of violence they can unleash. There are other toll collectors that are legal. They consist of local council officials and the landowner's children properly called *Omo Onile. Most of these omo' onile don't bother to do anything reasonable, they spend time harassing tenants and visitors. From shop owners, they collect daily levies at their discretion. Street traders are not also spared. Most times their wares are seized. Cart pushers are the worst exploiter. The weaker you are the more you are oppressed with brute force also not exempted from the collection. Every truck or trailer entering markets and even private vehicles entering the market are worst hit. The most irritating and vexatious is that most of the levy are not standardized. Most of the levies are named according to the prevailing situation. When there is theft engineered by same area boys, the levy becomes security levy. When trucks come into the park to off load goods, it is called offloading levy. When the truck comes into load goods, it is called loading levy. The name of the levy can change five times a day. Most of these levies are not receipted or ticketed except for the ones collected by local government officials.

Payment is not optional as there are several enforcement methods like physical mob actions and assault on the victim or damage to vehicle. The police stand there watching and forget it is their duty to maintain the peace of the society. The impact of most of these unreasonable levies have a ripple effect on the cost of transportation and other affiliated activities because in most cases the vendors build in the charges of the area boys. This has been the situation as long as the Reverend Father could remember. Shockingly the number of area boys in Lagos has been increasing through the years because some of the grown up Almajiri relocates to Lagos to pursue their dreams. Some result to driving motor cycles without any training and this explains the high number of motor cycle accidents on daily basis in Lagos. These grown up Almajiri who relocates to Lagos for greener pasture can neither read road signs nor understand the meaning of the symbols. Some of them are luckier. After riding motorcycle for some years they graduate to tricycle operators. Those are the few amongst them who try to live a good life. These ones don't take drugs or involve in criminal activities. They have semblance of religiosity, pray five times a day, forbid any intoxicants, live pious life, do not fight or take part in any negative violence. They are the direct opposite of area boys who are tools of urban fear. They are the worst night mere to anybody who encounters them.

Foreigners never stop wondering why a rich country like Nigeria will allow children of tender ages to be abandoned on the streets without plan of proper rehabilitation especially from the government. Governments in Nigeria have often dismissed the activities of louts as illegal, but have never made a lasting attempt to tackle the menace created by their existence most especially sending them off the streets. Although laws are set against thuggery, theft, collection of illegal tolls and levy, the law enforcement officials have simply made the laws ineffective because many of them are extortionists.

The Reverend Father who is the Chairman of the Catholic Rehabilitation Center and special task force of getting indigent youths off the street, recently wrote to the government through the ministry of youth development on the need to intensify law enforcement against miscreants in the state, and particularly pay attention on the area boys who operate without any form of limit.

Since the letter was written and several reminders sent to the administration of the government, some two thousand seven hundred miscreants have indeed been nabbed in separate operations. But in spite of this move, many areas in Lagos are still under the control of the area boys. However, in the case of Northern Nigeria, more Almajiri are produced and poured into the streets like libation and no plan has been made to stop the Almajiri system or reduce the situation. A school of thought believes that since the Almajiri system has great benefits to the wicked and unreasonable politicians they will negate against any move to abolish the system.

The behavior of the area boys in Lagos and the Almajiri in the north is and impediment on the socio-economic status of Lagos State and a serious embarrassment in the north.

Also life pressure and business environment in Lagos is a tasking one; it is made worse by the activities of area boys who work in partnership with local council officials to unleash more hardship on the already hard situation. This is unlike the north where the pressure is not much because of high level of docility and ruralization. Life is lived at a very slow pace here. The northern parts of the country would have been better to live if not for their barbaric tradition and culture.

The tragedy of the chaos created by these systems of Almajiri and area boys is that the politicians don't seem to care. It is sad to see that the total waste of human lives are not too different from a jungle scenario. The Reverend gentleman noted that the movements of delivery vans and trucks within the metropolis have become 'a nightmare', regretting that motorists groan under the weight of so many permits and licenses, with some vehicles having to display as many as 21 stickers and tickets on their windscreen! These are activities you cannot find in any country of the world except Nigeria. It is not surprising that a country with huge oil and gas reserve like Nigeria has this degree of human decadence. A visit to other countries with less natural resources make you dumb founded. To explain and show its diminishing state, a president of a neighboring African country once joked and said, 'After visiting Qatar and Dubai, he believes Nigeria is not selling crude oil but ground nut oil.' This statement reveals the contrast in the level of development in infrastructure and labour between Nigeria and other oil producing states. Since the country has refused to provide jobs for the area boys, they have resorted to creating jobs for themselves legal and illegal through revenue collection. Some of the 'mandatory' revenue are in form of licenses and permits like Lagos Drivers Institute License; Driver's License (issued by FRSC); Local Government Permit; Hackney Permit and Dual Carriage; Vehicle License; Certificate of Road Worthiness and Barge Permit. Others are: Conductors Barge; Vehicle Identification Tag; Vehicle Radio and Television Permit; Vehicle Outdoor Mobile Environmental Sanitation Permit; Nigerian Police Emblem; Lagos State Consolidated Emblem and Ministry of Transport Certification.

'Heavy duty vehicles and many other delivery vans don't go out of factory gates until very late in the day when they are sure Vehicle Inspection Officers (VIOs), Road Safety Corps and the local council officials have closed for the day.'

The Reverend Father stressed that while payment of tax is necessary, the way local government councils go about it is disincentive to business, especially when arbitrariness and harassments by area boys are employed. He explained that many organizations have suffered embarrassment as a result of requests by local council officials for so-called radio and television permit.

'There is a lot of arbitrariness with rates ranging from ₦30,000 to ₦200,000 per annum. On parking permit, many organizations have been served various charges ranging from ₦50,000 to ₦500,000 per annum depending on the location and number of parking lots. For companies in small and medium enterprise categories, these demands are very burdensome,' the reverend said.

'We appreciate the fact that the state government does not have direct responsibility over the administration of local governments, but we believe it can prevail on them for a moderation of the fees and regulate the activities of area boys, streamlining of the levies/permits, and proper coordination between the state and local councils. Information on approved rates and fees should be widely publicized to curb abuses and allow for better planning by businesses,' he added.

Suddenly, Fatimah fell to the ground. The Reverend Father quickly knelt beside her with her eye widely opened. 'What is your name?' he asked gently. Fatimah shrank back from him, her terrified eyes darting quickly to the driver.

'Her name is Fatimah,' the driver responded.

The reverend father looked at the driver. It is hard to tell how old she is. But he guessed she is not more than 15 years yet her life has been inflicted with much pain and turmoil. There is an air of hopelessness around her that wrenched the heart of the Reverend Father.

The Reverend Father's eyes scanned everywhere around him as they alight from the bus. He took notice of Fatimah. They all look like refugees as they alighted from the bus; extremely worn out and tired and looking lost and abandoned. Just then, the words spoken by his master nearly two thousand years ago were repeated in his heart,

I was hungry, you gave me no meat, I was thirsty, You gave me no drink. I was a stranger, and you took me not in, naked and you clothed me not {Mathew 25;42-43}.

He retraced his steps and stood looking at Fatimah,

'What is your name and what brought you to Lagos all alone?' he asked softly.

Fatimah looked away, as if ashamed to identify herself.

The reverend father barely heard the mumble, 'Fatimah.'

'Well Fatimah, wait here in the park let me get you food in a take away pack so that you eat before you start going to your destination, okay?'

Fatimah face lit with great anticipation. The driver shrugged. He will use the time to sort other things before he borders about helping her to get to her location.

'I will be right back,' the Reverend Father said as he walked towards the local food center in the motor park.

'My Lord,' he muttered, brushing the tears from his face. 'This girl is hungry and dirty and have lost all hope.'

He turned back to Fatimah, 'Where are your people? Are they coming to pick you?' At once, the bus driver interrupted, 'Please, Pastor, give this food as you promised her, so that she will have power to answer all your question. Her story is a very long one. It is not the type that is said on empty stomach.'

The reverend father hurriedly goes to the restaurant and shopped more carefully than usual, choosing food that will provide nutrition for several days. The he hurried back to Fatimah with plenty of food. He opens the plastic bag he put the food and spreads it on the ground beside the bench. The driver stretched out his hand to help him. Fatimah's eyes are anchored to the various type of food on the ground and the reverend father watches her with the corner of his eyes. The driver too longs for the food. The Reverend Father decided to offer him some which he gladly received and began the narration of the arm robbery attack on their way to Lagos.

He opened two packs of fruit juice, peeled back the flap on the milk carton, removed the wrapping from the paper plate, and said to her with a smile, 'Eat your food and be happy.' Fatimah did not even wait to observe the food before she begins to eat like a hungry lion who is finally feasting on his prey after many days of hunting.

More than a quick glance, her eyes stayed on the food as she ate voraciously. The driver felt tears in his eyes, *why will a beautiful girl like this be thrown to the wind?* he thought.

———»-0-«———

The driver tries to locate the house Fatimah applied with as a house help as he drives her quietly. He is going with her because it is her first time in Lagos. Hence, he wants to make sure that she is safe before he leaves her. He thinks about the night journey to Kaduna that he will soon embark on as he fixed his eyes on the road. He is also touched by the exceptional kindness displayed by the reverend father to Fatimah whom he just met. Now the driver too is determined to ensure she gets to her destination safe.

Locating the address was not an easy task as it took them about two hours before they saw the house which hides between inter winding streets. The driver pointed to the house from a distance and wished Fatimah good luck as he hurriedly turned to prepare for his journey back to Kaduna. Wind sliced across the open field, whipping Fatimah's hijab and wool scarf as she walked through the gate leading to the house. She started towards the veranda where some girls are soberly gathered and watched her walk towards them. A layer of dust formed over the veranda. Fatimah felt everyone in the house gazes at her as she moves towards the veranda. Some other ladies were watching from the gate behind her, and the madam in charge of the house stood out as if awaiting her. Fatimah was the lone figure walking across in the stillness of that afternoon. Every sound seems magnified; from the sound of her slippers, to the rush of her breath.

Fatimah emerged from the knot of personnel and came forward to greet the woman, called 'Madam' in charge of the house. Not responding to her greetings, the madam in a very harsh tone asked, "what do you want, girl?"

'Ma, I saw an advert in the newspaper that they want a house girl in this house. That is why I am here.' She responded, a bit jittery.

'Are you sure you are strong enough for this job?' Madam asked, looking at her in deep scrutiny.

'Yes ma, I have been doing it before.' she bent her knees in response.

'Okay, go inside,' she said observing Fatima's stature. She instructed one of the girls to take her inside and show her around. As Fatima makes her way into the house two more girls arrived and were all accompanied inside too.

Inside is like a congested hostel. Most Nigerian women leave their homes in hopes of a better future, but in reality become victims of a very organized and sophisticated net of human trafficking and sexual slavery. There are greener pastures but not everybody is fortunate to stumble on green grass. Sometimes when faced with little option, the biggest challenge is to make the right choice. To some life could be a bed of roses while to others life is a bed of thorns. Nigeria seems to be a bed of thorns for millions of youth who resort to fleeing the country. The girls, many of them under age, have often been promised jobs in Europe or any other white country but ended up in brothels. The sudden realization of being deceived put most of the girls in quagmire. They are deliberately treated like slaves to break their will and make them permanently dependent on their captors.

Fatimah is yet to comprehend what has befallen her and she has started wondering why there were so many girls in the house. Strangely, there is no male occupant except for the fierce looking security men outside which reminds her of the robbery incident on her way to Lagos. The girls came from different parts of the country. Some of them were tricked in the name of 'coming to work as sales girls,' after which they were locked up and camped without their family members knowing their whereabouts. While others like Fatimah unknowingly walked into the trap set by advertisement on papers for house helps. The modulus operando of this house is like a brothel run by a heartless woman who gives the girls to different man for money and prevent them from leaving and take all their earnings with constant promise of taking them to Europe to become hairstylists, house helps, and other befitting jobs to earn in dollars and rescue their families from poverty. This story line has been the major incentive for the girls to remain in the house without complains. When any of the girls goes out for *runs* and does not return back, the story told to the other girls is that they have gone to Italy or other parts of Europe for real jobs. However, some of the girls are truly shipped to Europe but what they go through in Europe is hidden from the rest who remain in Nigeria. The trafficked girls are made to take beautiful pictures in beautiful locations and sent to the house to convince other girls of the beautiful life that awaits them. This is done in the first few days of arrival before the girls understand the real purpose of their mission in Europe. Most of the girls are trafficked with illegal documents thus making their stay in Europe illegitimate and are forced to leave in the dictates of their traffickers who enslaves them until they are able to raise the money used to traffic them to Europe with the interest on the so called investment. The trafficked girls spent most of their time evading the local police in the country they are trafficked to. One key strategy in the house is that nobody ever leaves that house and comes back to tell the story to those left behind. Those left behind are made to believe that those who left had gone for greener pastures, only beautiful pictures are shared and pasted on the walls of the sitting room well framed.

Some girls whose pictures are lying on the wall showing high level of flamboyancy are indeed suffering beyond imagination on the streets of Europe. Margret Adebanjo a native of Oyo state in Nigeria was enticed by her neighbor to quit her hair dressing job and spent her savings on travel. They arrived this same house in

Lagos and commenced induction and orientation. After about two years she was smuggled to Italy but since she got there life has been a living hell but she was made to take pictures with flashy cars and beautiful apartments. Those pictures are sent to the house and pasted on the walls.

It was on a cold and windy evening. The trees swayed from side to side as if dancing to a sonorous rhythm of ebullience and exuberance proportion. Barn swallows were heard flying from trees to trees on this winter evening where temperature is two degrees centigrade. The typical winter cold was unbearable for most people making it intolerable to walk in the street at night and so cars are a rare sight to behold. Most families are in doors. Margret Adebanjo walks up and down the road, wearing a winter jacket and a red wig. The cold was beginning to have effect on her body as her teeth were already grinding each other. She has been patrolling the street for four hours. Although she still have enough strength to continue the hassle, her desperation has tremendously increased. Any day she came home without meeting the target, her freedom became farther. She must refund the thirty thousand US dollars the sponsors claimed they spent on transporting her to Europe. She had set a target for herself but today seems to be a very bad day as she could not get any customer. Suddenly her head starts spinning as she begins to have a faint spell. Feeling more and more lightheaded, she reached out to her bag and took out two tablets and quickly swallowed them without water and allowed spittle to accumulate in her mouth to push down the tablets. She became a little relieved but something was still wrong as she was missing her steps. Some Italian police officers who were on patrol noticed something was wrong. A car halted in front of Margret and drove her to the nearest police station.

Margret had all her documents and lied to the police that she was robbed and drugged knowing fully well she would be tested for drugs. She explained she was on her way to visit a friend when two huge men lured her into the bush and robbed her of all her money then drugged her. The police fell for her story and promised to take her to her destination. On the way, the interrogation continued. Margaret was reluctant to speak out but after a little persuasion she could not stop the flood of contradiction she was pouring out. "Yes. I came here because I was told I would work at a hair salon but as soon as I arrived, my passport was seized and I found out that there was no saloon job. I am forced into the streets looking for men to sleep with me for a pay. That is the only way to pay off the debt of the journey from Nigeria. I was brought here without a financial contribution from my side."

Margret has the same storyline with some girls and young women who are trafficked to Europe for sexual exploitation. Some of the girls are recruited at a very young age and had never experienced any sexual intercourse before leaving the country. They are deceived with death of their loved ones then forced into prostitution. The girls are responsible for their health, if any of them contract any disease, they are made to pay for the treatment from their wages.

They are bound by fear. Any of the girls being trafficked for prostitution are taken through voodoo rituals and their families stand as sortie. They are threatened and forced to put their wards in check. There is the belief that if any of the ladies renege on the agreement the voodoo curse would kill the person.

The abuse endured by Margret is a common fate for ninety-nine percent of Nigerian girls who reach Italy by sea. Virtually all the girls from Nigeria arrive Italy through water transportation and are all victims of trafficking for sexual purposes. The case of Nigeria is a tragedy of apocalyptic dimension. Nigeria has defied all sense of reason due to the fact that the country is one of the most endowed countries in the planet. The citizens of Nigeria are fleeing in droves to countries far less endowed with natural resources. A country where the people are deprived, depressed and subjected to highest level of corruption cannot deliver to her people the good things of life. Nigerian and other Africans fleeing to Europe risk exploitation from traffickers, starvation and shipwreck. Traffickers target younger and younger victims. The young girls are instructed and warned not to reveal the truth of their age to the checking authorities, so that they will not be transferred to a minor center, where it is more difficult to run away from, because of the very tight security and monitoring making it impossible for them to start working on the streets as sex workers.

Young boys and girls are the people who are most vulnerable of the migrant population that come to Italy by sea. The Mediterranean has become the water loo of some of the population that tries to cross it for greener pasture. This does not discourage or reduce the number of people still attempting to cross the Mediterranean. The pressure created from abject poverty created by animalistic politicians back home pushes the young people to continue the suicide mission. There have been many sordid and horrific stories surrounding human trafficking. The inhuman degrading process they are made to go through can better be imagined than experienced. But the sad reality is that the stories are all true. The experience of the trafficked sex slaves in Libya can best be compared to the life of animals in an unkempt cattle ranch or piggery.

A lady called Rose who was working in a local bakery in Lagos was promised a golden life in Italy. She gave the traffickers all her life savings to transport her to Italy with a promise that a very good job was waiting for her. They travelled by road through Agadaz, in Niger republic. After six days journey by land from Kano state in Nigeria to the Libyan camps in Misratah through the Sahara desert, many died on the way and were covered with the desert sand and their international passport placed on the top of the shallow grave. At a point they ran out of water and were drinking their urine. Only few of them managed to get to Libya. Their life In Libya was next to hell as they were put in a small room, males and females sleeping on the floor, packed like sardines. At night you could not move your body without interrupting or inconveniencing another person. It is expected that the guys will do menial jobs while the females will engage in prostitution to be able to raise the money for boat to cross the Mediterranean. For Rose, sexual slavery was something she only read happening to others in newspapers and at times heard them on radio. She never thought she would fall a victim. Rose would constantly remind herself bitterly, 'I left a mere coal of fire in Lagos, Nigeria, only to find myself in an inferno equal to hell.' Locked in a small hall with males and other females with one toilet, they are brought in food like a dog through the widow with iron protectors. the ladies are brought out and taken to a small room if there is a male customer while the males are locked up in the room except there is a dirty job to be done like clearing the drainage and washing the public toilets. Most of the time, the customers came in very drunk and dirty and forcefully have their way on the women. Any resistance from the forced sex worker is severely punished.

Libya is a gateway where all traffickers and people being trafficked from Africa going to Europe by road must stop over for months or years searching for money to cross over. For some, Libya is the end of their journey because it is difficult to survive human abuse and degradation in Libya. Even when they manage to survive Libya, crossing the Mediterranean is a suicide mission. Some of the parents die during crossing and the children are left orphaned. Many children and young people have to be separated from their parents left behind in Libya. Not having enough resources to pay for all the family members to cross to Italy, due to motherly affection, mothers try what they can to send their children to Europe first, in order to spare them a longer stay in a country where the life of migrants is a living hell daily subjected to daily violence and abuses and treated less than animals. This explains the large number of unaccompanied migrant children arriving Italy by sea. For an unaccompanied migrant child, too often, danger, abuse and even death is a reality they have to face.

The number of children arrivals is on the increase and higher than the overall number of migrants' arrivals. Majority are in their teens; some migrated to Libya for the golden fleece already being brainwashed to believe jobs can be gotten so easily having paid humongous amount of money to the traffickers. Others dreamt of going to Europe from the very beginning, but they fall all the same into the spiral of violence and abuses there. For those who did not plan to come to Europe in the first place, crossing the Mediterranean becomes the only way out to survive because of the living hell Libya had become. Then, there are the young girls who, mostly deceived with very alluring jobs, are made to abandon whatever they were doing back home and are trafficked. These ones fate was once sealed in their countries but who are psychologically manipulated by taking fetish voodoo oaths and then "escorted" to Italy with the sole aim of sex slavery.

Many of the trafficked victims get tired of the life of sex slavery and try to escape giving less concern about the deadly consequences. Lucia accepted the offer from a relative to help her go to Italy. She was made to believe she was entering a brighter future and subsequently rescue her family from poverty. She was an excellent hair dresser. The relative made her believe she will make more money in Italy fixing peoples' hair. She was just twenty-two years. The relative told her she must swear an oath to pay back all the money spent in taking her to Italy and she needed some good luck charms to attract customer and make a lot of money. The relative handed Lucia to the agent who took her to a bus park where she handed her a ticket and telephone number she will call when they get to Libya. The agent in Libya will handle the trip from Libya to Italy. Lucia arrived Kano and continued to Niger republic in a bus packed with young ladies and few men. They got to Libya after three tortious week. Lucia managed to get a phone and called the agent's number. A husky voice answered the call. He was a huge man who hailed from the Middle Eastern part of Nigeria. He instructed her to wait at the bus station and few minutes later he arrived. To Roses' surprise the whole group of people that they stood together in the bus station was waiting for the same man she was waiting for. He took them to a house and warned them to remain indoor until their boat was ready for Italy. After two months of confinement in the house, where she experienced severe beating and aggressive rape from the men of the house who were deliberately nasty and wicked. After much infliction of pain, Lucia and other migrants who joined them later were taken to the shore where they were to board the boat. It is obvious that the safety of the boat is the last consideration for the desperate migrants. All they want is to cross the Mediterranean into Europe for greener pasture. The boat was over loaded, carrying far above the capacity it was designed to carry. The boat set sail and the horror began almost immediately. Screams and shouts rented the air as the boat wavered seriously and water started entering the boat. The sailor did an emergency U-turn back to the shore. One third of the passengers were disembarked. It was not easy as no passenger wanted to come down. Lucia was lucky to be among those the boat carried. This time around the boat sailed without any mishap. The passengers were exactly the maximum number the boat can carry. They arrived Sicily quite late and went straight to the apartment of the biggest human trafficker in Italy, a Nigerian woman who has escaped justice by subterfuge both in Nigeria and Italy. She parades herself with multiple identities. She called all the ladies and asked them to sit on the bare floor while she sat on one of the chairs reeling out the dos and don'ts. She gave the women some clothes and condoms and literary told them that they were here for prostitution and that they had to earn a minimum 100 Euro per day so that they can liquidate the debt of 30,000 Euros, the amount used in shipping them to Europe. They were not allowed to go the house of any client without a prior knowledge of their supervisors. They were to bring their 'clients' to a detached house within the vicinity they were staying and give all their earning to the supervisor who in turn gives them a receipt to acknowledge the payment. They keep dual records until the debt is fully paid. Within the short period of arrival in Italy, Lucia was put under unimaginable duress to work, trading only on sex on the streets and when there was no work, they were locked up in the house. A typical work day began at ten in the morning until nine at night, and after a few hours of rest, they were back on the street for the late night shift, from after midnight until six in the morning. Lucia could not imagine her continuation in this horrendous life style of sleeping with an average of ten to twelve men in a day. She decided to plan a way of escape, and she started hiding some proceed of her prostitution trade. After three weeks, Lucia left the house for work as usual but instead of heading for her location of prostitution, she headed for the train station heading for Rome. She was given an address of a place to go to in Rome. On arriving Rome, she went straight to the place where she was given but she was shocked it was an overcrowded detention center. She was later told they would be deported to Nigeria. Rose said to herself, 'I have moved from frying pan to fire. Go back to Nigeria? Never!' Some women also shouted in anger while others cried. Lucia, however, maintained a stoic silence, 'I walked into this trap myself and I will walk out unnoticed too.' There was a lawyer from a voluntary organization standing by the entrance of the center. Lucia walked up to him and narrated her story informing the lawyer that if she was deported to Nigeria, the trafficking gang would kill her. The lawyer took up her case and made an asylum application for her. That would allow her to remain in Italy and after a few more weeks she was transferred to a migrant center in central Italy to wait for the processing of her case.

Lucia was extremely traumatized and dehumanized. Like most victims of trafficking, she was in terrible shape and totally desponded. These people have seen hell and they are managing to survive day by day. Many school of taught cannot comprehend the motivation for human trafficking except greed and evil nature. Why will a human being take pleasure in the dehumanization of their fellow human beings? The root cause of human trafficking is extreme poverty caused by bad government riddled by incompetence and corruption. Nigeria is a country that has no reason to be poor with an avalanche of Natural resources. It is the only country in the world that has crude oil and large deposit of gas yet still very poor. Majority of trafficked victims in Europe are women, mostly from Nigeria and other parts of western Africa. Many are subjected to sexual violence and other abuses throughout their journey. As many as two-thirds of them are forced into prostitution and are enslaved by their traffickers upon arrival.

Many migrant women were trafficked are disconnected from any source of help. Every movement is kept secret from the migrants until the last minutes so it is almost impossible for them to seek help because they are not able to escape from their traffickers again. Most of them are very naïve or they don't know how to seek help because of the language and cultural barriers. Human trafficking for sexual purposes has become one of the most profitable illegal businesses that violate human rights.

Many don't even know that they are being trafficked because initially they are deceived to believe they are going for greener pastures. When they eventually understand that they are being trafficked they don't even know that trafficking is a crime. They know they have suffered violence and abuse but they don't know that they are victims of an international crime and that as victims they have rights to legal recourse. Lucia was deceived, abducted, beaten and exploited for forced labour. The summary of her experience is *profoundly abusive forms of exploitation.*

The movement of Nigerians to Europe and other parts of the world is motivated by the belief that there would be financial buoyancy. Because of this, many of them forged their documents to get there. The ladies end up as prostitutes while the guys go for odd jobs because finding regular jobs require the right documents with legal status in the country. Many Nigerian families saved and even borrowed money to send other children to Europe because of total despondency. Benin City, a notorious State, is noted for the highest number of trafficked victims. Some parents sell their houses to send their daughters to Italy. This situation led to the creation of a new dimension of human trafficking where the traffickers help potential victims get to Europe and sell them to European traffickers who are also Nigerians who have been in Europe for a long time. These people are nicknamed 'Landlords.' Most of them are supposed to be in prison but have devised a way to escape the law. The victims, who are mostly women, arrive the foreign country with huge debts to pay their agents who have used their own money to ship them to the European or whatever part of the world they find themselves. They are forced to work in the brothel until their debts are repaid.

Periodically, the number of Nigerian women who arrive Italy by crossing the Mediterranean Sea from Libya is unimaginable. It is called the journey of death or a journey to tragedy. The stories are the same year after year, easily predictable. Targeted victims are women. Their will have been broken by humiliating poverty. They are ready to do anything for survival. The sponsors of the trafficking with alias like 'madam,' play the critical role in the recruitment and the financing of the obnoxious trade. These women who give an impression of undertaking legitimate business in Europe become the envy of the potential victims who want to be 'successful' like them. The 'madam' promises them lucrative jobs like hair dressing, and fashion sales girls and that they will earn foreign currencies which, when converted to local currencies, will be much. The frightening process of transiting to Europe through Libya and the suffering involved in the whole journey especially in Libya and the rate of boat capsizing in the Mediterranean has not been strong enough to discourage or reduce the rate of illegal migration. Most of the women who eventually arrive in Europe are survivors of the Libyan hell held against their will. They are dehumanized and are only allowed to leave Libya after months once they are able to pay the ransom demanded of them. They are completely conscious of the danger to cross the sea, but are willing to undergo the risks to end their Libyan nightmare because in Libya there appear to be nothing to live for as they are treated like non humans. The impression that the streets of Europe is laced with gold and that Euros are picked on the ground immediately disappear when they arrive Europe, mainly Italy and realizing that they have been deceived, they are moved to some reception centers. The Nigerian Mafia group responsible for the trafficking has already put a process in place to get them out and moving them to specific location where they are further intimidated and threatened to fall in line and are reminded that they have very huge debt tied across their neck which must be paid. Because of the presence of the Nigerian Mafia everywhere. These victims of traffic know that the traffickers will find them sooner or later if they try to be smart especially because of the presence of the Nigeria Mafia everywhere. The Mafia has all their documents, names and information about their families.

The most effective means of manipulating the trafficked victim is a *'vodoo'* ritual known in local parlance as '*juju*'. This is very common in West Africa and it has cultural backing. Most women coming to Europe are made to take an oath swearing that they will pay the entire debt and never denounce the traffickers. According to this ritual, they swear and place a curse using the name of the local deity that if they escape, they will die, if they tell the police the truth, they will die, their blood is involved in the oath taking. Although this is nonsensical and sounds like a superstition to the Europeans, in reality, it proved to be a much stronger manipulative arm to the Nigerian women than violence and aggression.

Because of this oath, all the trafficked victims are always dancing to the tune of their captors and as such they obey and do not dare to report to any authority or give any name or tangible information about the traffickers that will lead to their arrest or interrogation. They mainly focus on how to pay back the debt. They remain victims of sexual exploitation in a very dehumanizing way and even after paying the entire debt they remain in bondage because they don't have legal papers to stay in Europe and as such do not have legitimate jobs. It is extremely difficult to fully integrate into the society and find a regular job. The practice is that when you have finished paying your debt, you become a 'madam' of your own, either in the European country or you return to Nigeria where you are considered as a successful and respected person. Funnily, even government officials patronize their illegal businesses. They become so powerful that it becomes very difficult to fight against the human trafficking Mafia.

Gladys is a promising seventeen years old Nigerian girl who struggles to complete high school because her father does not sponsor or assist her schooling. Her poor mother managed to pay her fees from the little earning she makes from her petty trade. Sadly, the unimaginable happened. Gladys was raped by one of the government officials. When accused, he denied vehemently that he had no association with Gladys. The case was not further investigated. Of what usefulness would that be anyway especially for a common family in the society. As an adage goes, "the knife has cut the child, the child threw away the knife, but has the knife not done what it wanted to do? Even if the official was persecuted, could it have cured Gladys' protruding belly? Her father, being very angry, kicked her out of the house. Few years later, just a little above twenty-one, Gladys who is now a single mother, living in abject poverty, with no help coming from anywhere, was trafficked and exploited as a sex worker after being lured to Libya under the guise of a better job.

The eldest of nine children from a polygamous home, Gladys was just one of the thousands of young girls who are enticed by promises which, unknown to them will never be fulfilled but are in the long used by wicked and unreasonable 'landlady' or 'madam.'

Gladys is now thirty-one years old and back in Nigeria where she hired a room in one of Lagos deadliest ghettos. She narrates the hell she experienced in Libya, hoping that others, especially females will learn from her bitter experience and avoid the trap of being set by the callous traffickers. 'I was a very brilliant girl who had the dream of becoming an accountant. Although my father condemned my going to school because I was a female child, my mother supported and stood by me always until I was raped by a government official who was so powerful that he could not be probed…it means that we had to let sleeping dogs lie because we, my family I mean, was just a commoner in the society. The aftermath of the rape was unwanted pregnancy. My father, who even cared less of me because I was a female child, threw me out of the house and my poor mother, my mum, had no power to stop that from happening. I lived with my mum's relation for some time before a man introduced me to a woman who promised to change my life. She told me that I will be going to Italy to get a good job that will bring plenty of money for me to take good care of my child and my mother. She gave me a lot of gifts. I had no cause to doubt her sincerity as money was radiating all over her. In fact, everything about her reveals affluence and abundance.'

When she returned to Nigeria, Gladys started selling fruit and vegetables to keep body and soul. 'I didn't make enough money, but I was able to get enough to feed my child and send some support to my mum, some of my brothers and sisters.

'For almost a decade, I had no contact with the father of my son who was a very influential government official. He is the major factor to the abortion of my aspiration. It was when it dawned on him that none of the women who had children for him gave him a male child that he became frantic to get in touch with me.

'In Africa, there is preference for the male child because as it's their culture, he will continue the father family name. Most families hardly educate the girl child especially in the northern parts of Nigeria. As the father of my son was making frantic effort to locate me, my father fell sick. To his surprise, all the male children from his numerous wives could not come to his rescue because they have their own families to deal with. I was contacted after almost twelve years of silence from my family. I used all my savings to pay all my father's medical expenses and it got to a point I went into debt. My father and I became very close. His eyes was full of regret for how he treated me and the other daughters. Funnily, it is those girls he refused to train and care for that stood by him and cared immensely for him.'

The influential government official eventually linked up with Gladys and made all effort to make amends for the pains he caused her. He got her a new house and offered to pay all her bills henceforth.

'I didn't want to move to the house he hired for me but the situation was becoming more and more difficult,' Gladys says. When she recalls what she had gone through in life, it becomes extremely difficult to forgive this man who initiated her travails. She agreed to the Libya offer because of frustration and despondency. She thought she could change the life of her loved ones if she traveled abroad. Gladys left her son under her mother's care and reached Libya by road. She arrived in Tripoli, the capital city of the country, after a thirteen-day journey. She was sheltered in the backyard of a big house, in a room she shared with other young girls. This place was different from the detention center where they were severally abused. No one was abuse unnecessarily except if one refuses to cooperate with the dirty instructions.

'There were eleven Nigerian girls. They welcomed me nicely. They spoke well of the 'Madam' and advised me to obey her in everything she asked me to do,' Gladys says. 'When I talked about the work I was promised, the girls guffawed. They advised me not to ask 'Madam' about the work or else I will be taken to detention center where I will be broken totally to submission. Secondly, being in this place is a favor because there will be no physical torture or manhandling once you obey all instruction. "You have to pretend to be happy," one of the girls told me.

'The 'Madam came to see me every evening and asked me to rest. I was not allowed to go out and we were watched by a guard who hardly closed his eyes to sleep. The other girls were taken out every night to satisfy the sexual urge of some rich Libyan men who paid large sum of money to the 'Madam'. The first night I was taken out could best be described as awful and terrible! The Libyan man, who was my first client, wanted a *porta potty*. A porta potty is very common among the rich Arab men who pay between 25,000 USD to 50,000 USD to have sex with the ladies and poo directly into their mouth and pee on their face. Some are made to have sex with animals while the rich men watch. There are big stories of models agreeing to perform deeply scatological and fetishistic sex acts in exchange for the dollars. However in the case of the trafficked girls, the money goes to the 'madam.'

Gladys vehemently refused to participate in the porta potty and the Libya millionaire was livid with rage and beat her mercilessly. The madam was very angry and had to transfer her to the detention center where she was beaten, sold and sexually exploited for more than two years in Libya. Gladys longed of returning to Nigeria, her country of origin, to be reunited with her son and mother where she was managing her life before she was deceived. In the detention center, Gladys refused to be a sex worker except when she was raped. She was kept under surveillance.

'Madam used to come to see me regularly and insisted that I engaged in sex work for her. She said ladies with my body type are very attractive to the very rich customers insisting I am her investment and she must make returns on the investment. I refused and asked her to send me back to Nigeria. She told me that the only condition was for me to pay her back all the money they invested in bringing me to Libya.'

Gladys did not change her mind despite being deprived of food for a day, then two days. The woman ordered the other girls to convince Gladys and toughen the punishments meted at her. Madam looked at her and exclaimed "Gladys is dollars in motion!"

'I got slapped and severely beaten by the girls every night. I was locked and tied in a room when the girls went out for sex work. One of the girls who pitied my condition, explained to me that she, too, had been trapped in the same way and had ended up agreeing to be a sex worker because she needed to save some money for her escape at any available opportunity.'

Few weeks later, opportunity to escape came on a platter of gold. The government of Nigeria set a plan to evacuate all Nigerians stranded in Libya due to the outcry by international Humanitarian Organizations. In such case like this, when the government is involved, the traffickers go into hiding because human trafficking has been criminalized internationally. Gladys and her friends took advantage of this opportunity and went to the evacuation site which was heavily guarded by the police. Nobody can take you from the evacuation site by force. The number of people, especially men who hardly made enough money there, waiting for evacuation is very high.

Gladys and some other girls waited patiently in the evacuation center where they are offered food and medical attention although not on regular basis because for some days they didn't have supplies which made some of the girls went out for some fast work as the delay in evacuation to Nigeria increased and became frustrating.

Then Gladys agreed to be a temporal sex worker for while she waited for the evacuation. This time, she was in full control of her client. Most of the clients were available on weekends~ Fridays and Saturdays. They had some apartments around the evacuation center where they paid some money to take their clients there for short times.

The center arranged travel documents for every evacuating individual, and international non-governmental organization took over to support Gladys' reintegration process which would begin immediately she returned to Nigeria.

There was the pathetic story of Joyce. She met a woman who promised her a domestic work in Libya which would earn her a 1000 USD. Joyce was very happy. When she converted the money to Nigerian currency, it was about seven hundred thousand Naira, and of course, this was more than enough to solve all her financial challenges. She became anxious of moving to Libya. In no time, the woman made arrangements for her to travel to Libya. After a long journey through the Sahara desert that looked like a journey in the land of the devil. For she witnessed an unimaginable cruelty, from unfavorable conditions of the weather and land to the watching of drivers and other men beat and rape women and girls. Some girls died on the way and thrown out of the moving vehicle.

Joyce arrived in Libya after many near death experiences only to find out that she has been deceived. The 'Madam', the king pin of the whole trafficking syndicate told Joyce to undress and have sex with some clients. Joyce was extremely shocked and infuriated and shouted at the top of her voice, "I was promised a lucrative job here in Libya not a sex work," The 'Madam' laughed mockingly, "What job can be more lucrative than a man climbing you and you have some hot dollars for doing nothing but enjoying yourself." Joyce stood her ground. Since she wouldn't agree, the 'Madam' locked Joyce in a room without food for a whole day and got her boys to beat her mercilessly, threatening to kill her if she remained stubborn. She told Joyce to refund all the money she spent to bring her to Libya and eventually Joyce had no choice but to yield to Madam's desire as it was obvious she was going to be killed. The 'Madam' brought in men to sleep with her and other girls without any contraception or prophylactic. Sex without condoms attract a higher fee. Madam was only concerned about money. Whenever Joyce and two other girls became pregnant, they were forced to abort the pregnancy and the cost of the abortion is deducted from the girls' wages.

One day, Joyce laid on the floor helplessly, thinking about her trauma and exploitation. She confirmed suffering from physical and psychosocial health problems and that she sometimes thought of killing herself. She was an unhappy woman in the Madam's house. Food was never enough. Her future was uncertain.

When the Madam walked into the room, Joyce said with hurt, 'You think I am already dead by the way you passed me by.' The madam looked at her with utter shock when she spoke those words from the ground she was laying, 'I have had to wait for a time like this when you will be a bit calm for me to speak with you. I know

I have shocked you and treated you very badly but you see, I never forced you to come here. You chose to come on your own and I don't want you to hurt yourself by continually refusing to play by the rule and...'

Joyce interrupted rudely, shouting hysterically, 'You deceived me. You good for nothing woman!'

The woman looked at her funnily, 'It is obvious you are very unreasonable and you want me to lose my investment. But that's not possible you know. You will pay me back my money or you will pay with your life, you witch!' She stopped. She wanted Joyce to digest what she has said. After a few moments, she angrily walked out of the room.

The Madam could not cope with Joyce' resistance. Since all the cruel treatment meted out to her to die didn't work, she decided to sell her to another trafficker, a Nigerian man in Libya who was one of the most notorious traffickers with connections with the local Libyans. In order to escape from the law, he camps about four girls in his house claiming they are his wives. The local randy rich Libyans who were majorly his clients came in as his guest and they slept with girls after they have paid him handsomely. After some time, he would sell them and buy new girls. He used to select only beautiful and attractive girls and would spend a lot of money to upgrade them as part of his investment.

The man fully exploited Joyce. When she got to his house, he drugged her and raped her on daily basis until she had no choice but to cooperate. She left herself to providence with the notion of *what will be, will be.*

Joyce woke up one morning with an awful premonition that the man who had held her captive was going to do something about her constant incarceration and abuse. She did not want to get into trouble again. They all have common reason for their wicked actions- to make money and more money. Knowing that she needed to pretend to be happy and plan an escape, Joyce decided to go to the anti-trafficking center but the issue was how to get there safely without being noticed by the trafficking Mafia. It seemed luck was on her side. Surprisingly, one of her Libyan clients, who she deliberately pleased extraordinarily told her he was going to help her escape from the Nigerian man if she would keep it secret. The Libyan man gave her money intermittently and she continued to please the man hoping that one day she would be free from her captor.

'Hello,' the Libyan man's deep voice and pleasant smile nearly made Joyce forget that she was going to ask him how he was doing and how his day was going.

'It is very great and I have been thinking about you.'

Joyce felt herself blushing and wished she had better control of herself as the Nigerian man was suspicious of the seemingly familiarity between two of them.

'I came because I want to spend the whole day with you," he said. Joyce' eyes were watchful. She needed to gauge how she was going to respond to avoid any suspicion from the Nigerian man who by this time was getting too uncomfortable with the likeness the Libyan client is having for Joyce because this could spell doom for his business. The Libyan man looked intently at him and said, "I want you to know that she is a slave and have no choice so please stop all this nicety.'

After the Libyan man extricated Joyce from the Nigerian man by subtle threat and light coercion she moved into a house where the Libyan man was taking care of her as a mistress. This did not go down well with the Nigerian man who later caused indignation and highlighted the existential threat to their business to other traffickers.

On one Saturday night there was a lactiferous attack by the insurgent extremist armed group, Islamic State (also known as ISIS). They killed so many people and abducted the ladies including Joyce. They took Joyce to an underground prison and forced her to marry a man who raped her almost on a daily basis and Joyce thought the night mare would be sempiternal.

A year later, there was a capture on the ISIS camp and Joyce was among the lucky inmates who escaped to freedom. The Libyan soldiers helped her escape. She knew it was time to go back to Nigeria so she submitted herself to the International Organization for Migration (IOM) who then repatriated her to Nigeria. Joyce joined the anti-human trafficking volunteer organization, campaigning against human trafficking. She believed that God spared her life for the purpose of educating the others on the inherent dangers of illegal migration.

Doris was a young woman who was deported from Turin, Italy to Nigeria, Benin City after spending nine months in captivity in a rundown brothel.

She was arrested by the Italian security forces and

deported to Nigeria. After a fight broke out between her and one of her clients who accused her of stealing his money after drugging him. She was lured by traffickers into leaving Nigeria with promise of good jobs She became desperate to escape dire economic hardship and abusive family environments. Her father was married to seven women with almost forty siblings and none of the children had formal education. They even barely ate. Every day was turbulent in the house. Most unfortunately for Doris is that she was trafficked by a person very close to her who preyed on her desperation, making false promises of employment, professional training, and education. She was transported within and across national borders, often under life-threatening conditions.

Doris recounted the terrible journey. Traffickers forced her and other girls through the Sahara Desert to Benghazi in Libya, as a stopover on their way to Europe via the Mediterranean Sea. Their journeys were wrought with death, rape, beatings, fear, theft, extortion, and lack of food and water. Initially thirty two of them left Nigeria, only less than twenty five got to Libya and only six of them arrived Italy safely. Many died or got missing on the way. It was a journey you would pray for death. You cry until you cannot cry any more. People die, faint, are beaten, raped. In the journey, while almost leaving Agadaz, they were attacked by bandits. In the process, some died while some others were raped and beaten, and all of them were robbed. Doris kept on saying she would not advise even her worst enemy to travel by land. Only few people survive to tell the story.

Doris recounted how many women and girls are exploited in the forced prostitution network and various forms of forced labor, especially forced domestic work by their traffickers. The worst of all is that when these Nigerian ladies are raped and they conceived, they are forced to undergo abortions in very pitiable condition. No consideration is made concerning the sanitation or the risk of dangerous infection, and they are not given any pain medication. The trafficked ladies who manage to get freedom from their captives are subjected to another circle of humiliation. They face racial discrimination, arbitrary arrest, physical molestation and detention without any reason. They are denied the right to life and existence, living at the mercy of the whims and caprices of the society. The level of cruelty meted on these ladies is better imagined than experienced.

Doris recounts a day a rich client told her he wanted to urinate inside her mouth and she must swallow all the urine. When she refused, the client called her captor who punished her severely and the client ended up urinating on her face after having sex with her. This type of inhuman degrading treatment is a normal norm to these traffickers. The Madams subject trafficked women and girls to forced prostitution for long hours with no time to rest as they consider time as money and make them have sex with customers irrespective of their health. Even when they are menstruating, pregnant, or soon after childbirth or forced abortions, they continue their sex job. In some cases, the madam did the unbelievable and unimaginable. She would instruct the ladies to put sanitary materials, such as mattress foam or wipes, in their vaginas to block menstrual blood or bleeding from abortions so that they could have sex with their customers. The frequent narration of the victims is like series of songs with same lyrics, 'We were promised. We were migrating for very high-paying overseas jobs such as domestic works, hairdressings, or hotel staff, but to our surprise, we are forced into prostitution.' With dashed hope of getting a good life immediately replaced with a harsh reality of conversion of promise of a better life to debt they must repay, a debt they knew nothing about nor ever negotiated. Most times, this debt is determined by the Madam and imposed on the trafficked victims. Getting the victims to pay this debt is not a problem. The girls stand as collaterals and payback is enforced with maximum violence, threats, and retaliation against them or their families back home to control them. They also described traffickers' threats of selling them to other traffickers, surveillance, passport confiscation, confinement, and isolation to keep them trapped and terrified, and to avoid law enforcement detection. Apart from terror and compulsion, the most effective way the madams use to entrap the girls is by forcing them to undergo juju rituals or voodoo oats, frightening traditional oath-taking rituals that usually involve human parts of the victims like blood, finger nails, pubic hairs and clothes already worn by the victims. Although seen as superstition but the action compel the women and girls to pay their debts and not report traffickers to authorities.

Majority of the trafficked girls and women end up in fiasco. On return to Nigeria, many of them end up as emotional wreck, struggling with depression, anxiety, insomnia, flashbacks, aches and pains, and other physical ailments that have sometimes limited their ability to work effectively. They come back broke even worse situation than before. They embarked on the ill-advised search for the Golden Fleece which turned out to be a bitter mirage. For some, their suffering is worsened by families who blamed them for the abuses, ostracized them, or complained that they returned without money.

It was about 10:30 pm on the busy street of Catania Sicily. The street was packed with prostitutes. There were so many girls that a man just need to come and choose like the way you go to the market to pick a commodity. African sex workers are treated as merchandise. They live and die outside the law, imported for their bodies, and the women are trapped, traded and abused. For the madams and traffickers, everything is about money. The majority of the victims came from circumstances beyond their control.

Among these prostitute is a very beautiful thirty-two years old Nigerian lady who went to France few years back knowing she would be obliged to sell sex but was unaware that the debt she would have to pay was 45,000 USD. After some years, she was able to pay. But she fell very ill. The sickness appeared to defy the sophisticated European medicine so she had to go back to Nigeria empty handed. Her family was ashamed of her because she came back empty handed. After some years in Nigeria hassling, she was able to come back to Europe this time, Italy. While she was in France working for a Madam, she spoke of her experience, "My stomach was paining me and I suspected it was my period. I told the Madam I could not work for the day that it was my period but she shouted at me and called another girl to stick a wet tissue into my private. It was very painful and she pushed me out to go and meet clients. The madam can call you at any time to meet a client. She could call you on phone and say, 'Hello, where are you? Just give one shot and come back here and meet somebody else.'

One day I came home tired after I have slept with nine men. I wasn't fine at all. I began to bleed. I was seeing my monthly period. I was in pain. But my madam still forced me to go with a guy even after knowing my condition. I felt so much pain. But I have to pretend to be fine to the client until I could no more bear the pains and I pushed him hardly from my body. Then the brutal reality downed on me, the man began to beat me and threatened to kill me for interrupting his pleasure at the expense of my pains. Two of my colleagues lost their lives in such similar manner and my madam wept not for their lives but for the loss of profit. My madam exert her power through extreme violence. She is a member of a Nigerian Mafia group. They control the neighborhood. They beat up the trafficked women to submission; no food; no water and are locked up for days.

This always make us to wonder where the law enforcement agency are as all these happen. The Nigerian Mafia, are they deliberately ignored? If the police want, they can track them and stop their atrocities. It can be done! However, as the situation is, the evil practices, or let's say businesses, remain 'crimes unpunished', a huge smuggling and human trafficking enterprise in a country where the state turns the other face and the victims are broken," Doris exclaimed.

CHAPTER SIX

Light in the tunnel

Fatimah's mind was made up. She muttered, 'I came to Lagos to work as a house help and not as a prostitute. Any man that tries to touch me, I will kill him without blinking my eyes. I have been hardened by the affliction of life.'

Very early in the morning the next day, even before the first cockcrow, Fatimah and one older girl secretly left the brothel. They took every step cautiously avoiding to be noticed by the security. A wonderful peace stole over Fatimah as she entered the house they were going. It was just behind the brothel they just left. The house recruits house helps for homes and offices. The woman of the house, on seeing Fatima and the girl, warned sternly, 'Hey girls, we don't take prostitutes here. We only take clean girls as house helps.' The two girls were embarrassed. 'Introduce yourselves,' she demanded. Fatimah and the other girl narrated their stories.

The owner of the house had a kind face and her voice was filled with sudden sympathy after she listened to their different ordeals. The older girl has a touching story. She is an eighteen year old girl whose father died when she was eleven. Her mother remarried but instead of enjoying a father in her stepfather, he abused her severely. She was later trafficked by a woman who deceived her with a job offer in a saloon in Lagos.

'I was in SSS 3. My mum used to struggle to pay my fees. There was never peace at home for me. My stepfather used to beat me because I rejected all his advances when my mother was not at home. He wouldn't allow me to play with his children and would even deny me food. Any time he has the opportunity, when I am alone he tried to touch my breast promising me that if I cooperate with him, he would take care of me but as I remained adamant, he made his house a living hell for me. He would not allow my mum to continue paying my fees and told her to send me away. But mummy rejected. She said she cannot chase me away. The family was so abusive that succumbing to trafficking was the only option of escape. When the pressure became too much on my mother and my stepfather threatened to file for a divorce, I had to leave the house with the woman who promised me a beauty salon job. She brought me here to work as a prostitute instead of the saloon saying that it would fetch me more money. When I refused she took me to the house where I met Fatimah. She did not feed me. I ate nothing in the morning; they said I would eat when I learn to obey instruction. I also did all the housework. She beat me and abused me verbally. She complained I did not work well. I was always hungry but it didn't mean that I would stop working.'

⎯⎯⎯⎯⟫-◦-⟪⎯⎯⎯⎯

Fatimah was given to a rich family, the Williams, in Lagos as a house help. She wanted a family that would allow her to go to evening school so that she would complete her education.

Life in the Williams household is very different from anything Fatimah has ever known. Although there was always much work to do but she had so much to eat. There was plenty food in the house and Mrs. Williams was very kind to her and hardly beat her. But it seemed that trouble was brewing because Mr. Williams had begun to be sexually attracted to Fatimah and he started sending proposition to her and threatened her that she had to do whatever he wanted, because she belonged to him.

Sometimes after this proposition, Fatimah tried to run away from him.

Fatimah tried to make her life in the Williams' household bearable, but as Mr. Williams's sexual interest in her became very obvious as it appeared he lost every sense of self control, Mrs. Williams's takes out her jealousy on Fatimah. Mrs. Williams interrogated Fatimah about her relationship with her husband and always locked her up in the visitors' room and kept the keys to the room with her anytime it was night. Many times, Mr. Williams would crept from his bed to go to

Fatimah's room when Mrs. Williams was fast asleep but always got disappointed that the door was locked. One day, he confronted Fatimah, 'Why do you always lock yourself in your room every night?'

'Sir, I am not the one who always lock the room. It is mummy.'

'Why?' He asked, gazing through the gown she was wearing. He stretched his hand to touch her body but she fearfully ran off to the kitchen. Mr. Williams was unashamed and frequently berated Fatimah for being unyielding and unreasonable.

Mrs. Williams thought of a way to keep Fatimah out of the reach of Mr. Williams. She decided to enroll her in a school near her shop so that when she was going to the shop in the morning, she would drop Fatimah in the school and when she closed from school she would come to the shop and in the evening they would go home together. Mr. Williams suddenly refused to concede to the idea of Fatimah going to school. Moreover, Mr. Williams was not willing to spend any extra money on another man's child who is not related to him. Furious that his wife was deliberately creating serious gulf between his desire for Fatimah and Fatimah, Mr. Williams threatened to send her out of his house eventually, fearing that with the way things were going, he would never have access to the girl.

Mr. Williams' behaviour was especially pernicious to Fatimah who had been subject of not only physical abuse but also illegitimate sexual advances, and had no legal or practical means to protect herself. She was however thankful to Mrs. Williams who never stopped watching and guiding her from Mr. Williams who was unashamed to have illegitimate affair with a little girl he was old enough to be her grandfather.

Mr. Williams began to think of getting Fatimah out of the house and replace her with a more 'mature' girl. Fatimah is the seventh girl who had worked in the Williams household in the last two years. It is either Mrs. Williams pushes them out because they are in an intimate relationship with Mr. Williams or Mr. Williams pushes them out because he cannot get them on his bed. The common method Mr. Williams uses is to accuse them of theft. It is either he tempt them by leaving huge sums of money carelessly for them to steal or by intentionally putting the money in their bags. For Fatimah, it was becoming very difficult for him because Fatimah's honesty was too obvious and Mrs. Williams was so impressed by her behaviour. Mr. Williams knew that without his wife in the vicinity Fatimah would be completely powerless. He became desperate and decided to take action as fast as he could.

One day, Fatimah returned from the shop with Mrs. Williams and they saw Mr. Williams turning the house upside down, scattering everywhere under the guise that his gold wristwatch was missing. They ransacked the whole house until he got to Fatimah's room and suddenly shouted 'I have found it. Picking the wrist watch and marching gallantly towards Mrs. Williams and Fatimah, he started raining all kind of abuse on Fatimah, calling her unprintable name. 'Out of my house!' He shouted continuously. Fatima was totally stupefied and confused. Mrs. Williams was angry with her husband, and firmly said to his face, 'I would rather see you out of this house instead of Fatimah,' Mrs. Williams took Fatimah into her room and provided her a refuge totally from Mr. Williams who surprisingly watched them walked out on him. The silence of his wife to the accusation of the theft was very shocking to him because she has zero tolerance to any form of stealing.

Life continued for Fatimah in the Williams. The best part of her difficult life has been the one in the Williams house especially because of Mrs. Williams care and protection towards her. Before now, she had always prayed vehemently for death because of the hardships she faced. Now she knows she has to stay alive and make the best out of life because of the love Mrs. Williams showers on her. Undoubtedly, she becomes the best student in the school and hopes to get the school scholarship if she maintains her performance.

Because Fatimah still refuses to sleep with Mr. Williams, he makes her life miserable in the house. Her work in the house became more difficult, getting the house ready before going to school and later went to the shop with Mrs. Williams was daily sabotaged by Mr. Williams. For the first time Mrs. Williams wanted to get the perspective of Fatimah. She wanted to understand the travails of her young mind and to fathom the extent of the pains. She called Fatimah to her room and asked,

'What is the real problem between you and my husband? You have not told me what my husband did to you or why he hates you this much?' Fatimah was silent for some time, then suddenly she opened up,

'Ma, I have received unimaginable betrayals all through my life. These acts of betrayal were executed by people, who were once the closest people to me. I have been through a lot. I have seen hell and haywire. I am going to share my personal story with you.

'My parents planned to marry me off to a man I had never met in my life, a man old enough to be my grandfather. This was the beginning of my travails. I have slept in motor parks. I have stayed days without food. I have escaped rape and different forms of sexual assault. I know I am still on the run. Above all, I am claiming my right to preserve my own legacy, identity, and the true essence of the woman I am. I am determined to make it in this life, I will go to school, and thanks to you Ma for being a positive contributor to my life. I promise myself that I will go back and fight the evil system in my place. I sincerely believe my dreams will come true even if I have to always walk through the valley of the shadow of death. It was only God's grace that brought me to your house. Ma you are indeed God sent. Thank you for accepting me into your house. Ma, I have told you about my past but talking about your husband would be extremely disrespectful. It is better the issue is buried in sand of forgetfulness, please.'

'For your age, you have been through a lot,' replied Mrs. Williams in a very sorrowful voice. There was a golden silence. Few seconds later Mrs. Williams said again, 'I will support you and make sure you achieve your dreams, Fatima.'

For some weeks Fatimah hid from Mr. Williams and he also noticed the girl was avoiding him. He began to pour out his indignation on his wife. He would say, 'So, you have chosen this stupid girl over your husband!'

Mrs. Williams decided to send Fatimah to live with her cousin few meters from their house and pleaded with her cousin to allow her continue her education.

Sometime after Fatimah's departure from the Williams' house, a family friend named Beatrice who had admired Fatima asked about her from Mrs. William when she didn't see her in the house. Mrs. Williams opened up to her the challenges the little girl was facing from her husband and because she didn't want anything to affect the poor girl's very good academic performance she decided to send her to live with her cousin. Beatrice felt compassion for Fatimah and offered to give her scholarship until she graduated from the university. She demanded that Fatimah be brought to her house as an adopted daughter. Although Beatrice has nine sons but no daughter. She saw this as an opportunity to have a daughter she never had.

After an emotional farewell to Mrs. Williams, life became a bed of roses for Fatimah. The kind of life she had never experienced in her entire life is thrown at her on a platter of gold. Beatrice, her new mother, turns out to be very kind and sympathetic. Her opposition to inhumanity always make Fatima remember Dr. Amina, her hero. She offers to Fatimah every opportunity she gives her biological children.

Time marches on until it started to run. Seconds became minutes, minutes became hours, hours became days, days became years, Fatimah finished school with a historic grades and earned scholarship to study law in United Kingdom. Mrs. Williams kept track of her progress and supported Beatrice to take care of Fatima at every stage as a joint project.

It was now time for Fatimah to travel to the United Kingdom. A send forth party was planned by Mrs. Williams. The party was held in the Williams' house. It was a very emotional moment. Fatimah was made to sit at the middle of the sitting room surrounded by invitees. Mrs. Williams gazes at Fatimah's face. She was overwhelmed. Glittering tears fell from her wet, sparkled eyes. She burst into tears, letting out all the mixed emotion that bottled up deep inside her heart. The feeling of nostalgia, happiness mixed with sadness, and deep love not intentionally developed but came naturally. It's late when Beatrice realized that tears fell out of her eyes too. The more she tried to control herself, the more the teats kept pouring down her face. She walked out without a word to the corridor where she let go all her feelings.

Later that night, Fatimah was taken to the Airport and flew to United Kingdom to begin a new phase of her life.

CHAPTER SEVEN

Barbarian and primitivism

The barbaric culture of the abandonment of the male child turned ALMAJIRI continues unabated. Plates placed in their hands to beg for survival when they were much younger and naive no longer sustain them as they get older. Many of them, from the age of fifteen, seek another route of survival. The easiest route for them to escape the hardship of life is to align with rebellions like Boko Haram, ISWAP and many other terrorist group which take advantage of them. The greater part of the Almajiris now become the harvesting ground for the Boko Haram, and the ones who are not recruited by Boko Haram become bandits, forming their own groups or cells and taking over the different forests in the northern Nigeria. Their works in the country are to kidnap, rape, invade villages, engage in arson, shooting and cattle rustling, kill, and loot villages. The Almajiri turned Bandits are very brutal and merciless, often terrorizing communities in the North West region, ripping young girls out of the hand of their mothers, forcefully taking women irrespective of their marital status. The activities of Bandits in Nigeria rampage the whole society. They ride into villages with motorcades or motor cycles which have become a very profitable venture for them raiding hundreds of millions from their victims. The bandits are in hundreds of thousand controlling under-governed spaces where the government's control is ineffective and limited. The inability for government to curb the situation and the amount of money paid as ransom to them to release kidnapped victims are major factors that increase the bandits and grant them courage and strength to eat deep into the country. The forests are segmented and administered by different leaders. There is a strong bond and understanding among the bandits.

ISWAP is one of the tools which infiltrate the bandits, providing them with arms and ammunition and guiding them stealthily. ISWAP assists them with specialized personnel like bomb makers and intelligence advisers. The activities of the bandits and terrorists have displaced many people. Training camps for terrorists are not permanent too making it very difficult for the government to seize them. Thousands of women are kidnapped by these evil ones and taken to the camp for forced marriage and children that are born there are a product of rape on daily basis.

———⟫-◦-⟪———

September 1th was a dreadful day. The sky cried

profusely and thunder clapped at interval. It was as though the heaven was giving a warning to the people of the earth that the world was about to come to an end. The evening was dark. The noise of bombs drowns the sound of the rain. Cries and wails filled the whole inhabitants of a community which is administered by the Boko Haram. This is how it has always been since the terrorists and bandits took over the Northwest of Nigeria and decided to deny rest to the people. Among the wails and cries is a deep and piercing one that created more fear in the heart of the inhabitants. This time, it wasn't the fear caused by their attackers but the one of compassion. It was the cry of a new born baby.

Ahmed Salim was born into a world of violence and a fragrant display of man's inhumanity to man. Ahmed's mother, Fatima, who lost her mother in the course of this endless violence in the region, was barely sixteen when she was kidnapped two years ago from her school. She became the fourth wife of a seventy year old Umar who was one of the bandits' leaders and the most dreaded of them all. On this day of her delivery, she was aided by local midwives who were also captured by the terrorists. This was the second child Fatima now has; the first child, a female, was just trying to take her first step.

⟶•◦•⟵

Ahmed Salim grew very fast. At seven, he had understood the meaning of violence and bloodshed.

Violence had become a normal life for young Salim. His dad, Umar, who by this time was seventy seven, told him they were doing it in the name of the God. He dared not question his father but his little mind could not comprehend why the God, whoever he may be, will require much blood and enjoy the killing of the innocent like the little infants who died by stray bullets and bomb blast. The bandits are always busy plotting strike after strike. The news is always filled with terrible kidnapping activities and invasion of whole communities. Violence never seems to stop.

When Ahmed Salem was eighteen years old the father passed on and was buried in the family compound. He started living with his uncle who was more radical and by extension very unreasonable. He was in fourth in command of the bandit leader, a very terrible one. As it's their culture, he married Ahmed's mother less than two months after the death of his father and treated her very cruelly. One day, Ahmed returned from the farm. As he was about to enter the sitting room, he saw two men talking to the uncle in very low tones. Ahmed greeted them and to his amazement, the uncle told him to get his clothes ready and follow the men. He told him he would be living with them in another place, a very far place which takes almost a full day drive.

Ahmed raised his brow,

'What about my farm?' he asked.

'Which farm are you talking about? Forget about your farm, you have a more important assignment do. Farming is good but there is a better way to life. You will become a strong man with a strong mind to work for God.' He paused and looked sternly at Salim Ahmed, who also stared back in awe. He said again,

'You are going for a special training. You are at the ripe age for the important training. You must leave at once.'

The uncle did not discuss this with Ahmed Salim's mother. He felt she has no say as a woman. When Salim went into the room to pack his few bags, the mother saw him and asked,

'Where are you going?' Ahmed Salim replied,

'I am leaving with those two men in the sitting room as instructed by uncle,' the mother was shocked and dismayed. She asked in a low tone,

'Which two men?'

Ahmed replied, 'The two men with uncle wearing very long and unkempt beard.' The mother went down immediately sobbing, knowing what those two men represented. Ahmed tried to console her but the uncle came into the room and dragged him out, sternly warning the mother to stay away from the affair.

Ahmed and the two men arrived the camp situated in Sambisa forest Northern Nigeria near the Chadian boarder. Most young men and boys who are brought here never ever set eyes on their families again. The people they meet in the camp become their new family. Most of the Almajiris are the majority of boys in the camp.

The training camp for the terrorist has a semblance of a full military formation. There, the trainees who are mainly under aged boys and few girls are taught the rudiments of destruction and brainwashed into believing that what they do is for God and if they die fighting in His, they have juicy reward in paradise. The ages of the trainees varies from seven to sixteen. Kids as young as seven are given guns and taught how to kill and bomb. Human life is nothing to them. Kidnapped men who are unable to pay ransom are used as training materials on how to kill or how to be suicide bomber. Bombs are wrapped around the waist of kidnapped person, the person is taken to a midst of other kidnapped people and the bomb is detonated while the kids watch, jeering in excitement. This training is designed to disvalue the worth of human life in the consciousness of the kid trainees thus hardening their hearts making them familiar with holocaustic experiences.

Ahmed settled in the camp but could not come to terms with the heinous atrocity going on there. The training routine was always in the dawn. As soon as they woke in the morning, the Imam led them in prayers which was a bit different from what he did back home. The prayer here included some curses on the government system whom they see as infidel because they encourage Western education and Western lifestyle allowing women to go to school, and they engage in chanting of war and jihad. After the prayer, the training and indoctrination begin every day and as part of the training, somebody must be killed. They are never in short supply of human beings for the killing demonstration. The first day Ahmed was to demonstrate the killing aspect of the training by shooting on the forehead, a kidnapped innocent boy. Ahmed feigned a very serious fever and was lucky to be exempted from the exercise. For weeks he pretended to be sick and vomiting. The doctors examined him but could not trace any sickness to him but assumed it was a mental distress as a result of his newness to the system. They believed with times he would get used to it. Many people who came to the camp at this age suffer the same problem. Hence, they are mostly taken through a different orientation. However, the situation at hand did not give room for such orientation as the demand for suicide bombers had increased to meet up with the request by various terrorist groups. There was a supreme leader, Majid Abdul Karim, in the camp whose words were laws that must be strictly adhered to. Majid Abdul Karim had a soft voice with a very deceptive look. Ahmed wondered what qualified him to champion the cause of their said God-given assignment. His lifestyle is the opposite of a godly person. A serial rapist and a blood thirsty drug abuser who showed no mercy at the slightest suspicion of disloyalty. A mere suspicion of disloyalty to the supreme leader of the camp can cost anybody his life. He had an unquenchable appetite for rough sex. The kidnapped girls are taken to him. He selected those who could satisfy his sexual urge. His activities resolved around praying, shouting out instruction from a distance, and idling with those ladies captured against their will or watching pornography.

The training routine has been very hectic and

rigorous for young Ahmed. He has partly succeeded in escaping the aspect of killing people because each time it gets to his turn he feigns sickness. The instructors, therefore, decided to concentrate on those who are serious in view of the urgency while people like Ahmed are being given time to get familiar with the routine.

Ahmed has a friend in the camp. They became intimate and act like brothers because they both realized that they shared the same view about the evil activities in the camp. They however keep their friendship secret and only talk to each other openly on an official level. Alhassan is right. The camp instructors are beginning to notice the unwilling and uncooperative attitude of Ahmed which will sooner or later land him in a very big trouble because his safety in the camp will no longer be guaranteed. This is more serious because if one has gone through the period of indoctrination and brain washing, there is no looking back. The news around the camp is not too good. Most people who come in at an older age of fourteen hardly believe in the suicide bombing. Therefore they need special treatment. They must be taken through a special hate imbibing process.

Alhassan looks at Ahmed and says, 'I am worried about you.'

Ahmed, who looks worried and downcast, replies, 'why?'

'Ahmed, it is becoming obvious that you don't believe in suicide bombing. You must understand that if you kill anybody for the cause of Allah, you are sure of a good reward in paradise.'

Ahmed looks at Alhassan curiously, 'I thought you were more intelligent than these brutes who are wasting human lives as though they can create a fly!'

'Ahmed listen, if you continue like this, they will kill you!'

Ahmed, looking into the space said, 'I don't think God takes pleasure in the death of innocent people. I mean, all these senseless killings, are you telling me the God who is described as the most merciful and the most beneficial approves the killing of innocent school children in the name of religion?'

Alhassan looks even more confused than Ahmed, 'But we are fighting the infidels for Allah's sake!'

'Alhassan …! Just look at you. Listen to yourself, man! Do you think God, who created the whole world as you call Him, cannot fight for Himself? Or do you think that if God wants everybody to have only one religion, He cannot do it? Is He so weak that he requires mere mortals whom he created to fight for Him? Where were these bastards when He was creating the world? Where were they when He formed them in their mother's womb before the devil took over their lives? My friend, Islam means peace. Are we now giving peace or violence? This is a contradiction, you know too.' Ahmed said, almost in tears.

'Hmm… well, Ahmed, I must confess this question always echoes in my mind too but I fear to even contemplate the answers,' Alhassan replied sadly in a very low tone.

'Alhassan, why do you lie to your heart? Why do

you not want your good mind to also tell you the truth?' Ahmed asked his friend in compassion. 'In your mind, you know this violence is not anchored and directed by God but by men without honour or even the grace of God upon them. As we speak, I am planning my escape from this hell called camp!' Ahmed said bitterly.

'Ahmed, please be careful ooo! If you are caught, they will kill you! Anyway, I will like to escape with you if your plan is foolproof.'

'Alhassan...hmmm. If I stay, I will die. If I escape, I will have a chance of living and fulfilling my dreams,' he said like a seer.

Ahmed poured himself a cup of water, remembering how he was forced out of his mother's arms that fateful day he was coming here. Ahmed smiled wryly. If he had heard beforehand that he would be coming to a place like this, he would have run from home. He never believes in the religious violence around him even when he was a very small boy, but he is always a ceremonial Muslim, going to mosque and praying at all times. His late Imam back home always taught him to love people no matter their colour or race or gender. He demonstrated his teaching by the number of orphans he cared for. However, since the Imam died, he had nobody to look up to except his uncle who is a direct opposite of his late Imam. He took over the affairs of Ahmed's life and tried to make him embrace hate and violence. Alhassan absentmindedly watched Ahmed gulp the glass of water. He peers out across the trees to the other side of the field and whistles and hums softly to himself, a strange, Islamic tune.

'Now, I think this is a safe place to escape from if we decide to go ahead with your plan,' said Alhassan.

'Exactly,' Ahmed said nodding his head, 'we have been here for many hours now and people are just moving about without looking at us twice. Nobody appears to be concerned about us or what we are doing or talking about.'

'They think everybody has been brainwashed into believing their lies. Let me tell you, there are three other boys of our age who are not happy with the suicide missions. They wonder why these evil men's children are not in camp like us. I am fully aware that the camp commander has over twenty seven children and no one of the twenty seven children is part the suicide mission whereas I am the only son of my mother. They want to sacrifice me. If it is true they believe in the paradise theory why not sacrifice their children for the bombing,' retorted Alhassan.

Ahmed nodding his head in agreement, said, 'Truth. Those who believe in a course should be in the forefront.'

Present Day...

It is just before dark, the camp commander emerges from the potter cabin and waits by the corner near the tree overlooking Alhassan and Ahmed as they stand. He watches as they talk and gesticulate. He wears a very long unkempt beard that makes him very fierce and rash. Most nights when the trainees have gone to sleep, stench in alcohol, he gets down on the ladies. Many of the mature trainee notice it in spite of the pretense he tries to put up as a saint.

As darkness comes to settle on the face of the earth gradually, two men walked up to join him.

One of them whispers, 'What are those two boys doing there?'

The commander makes a move to call them for questioning but the other man holds him back,

'No wait, let them not disturb us. We need to get down to business.'

The camp commander, his senses sharpened by years of different kinds of living and violence, was smart to get the message. Those two guys have brought some drugs for the suicide bombers and this consignment is offered at very good price. He needs to settle the price before they changed their mind. The two men that brought the drugs are in their mid-forties. The younger one looks like a prosperous businessman looking at the diamond stones on his neck. But he is one of the ruthless drug barons plying his trade in Asia and Africa. He has been in this line of business all his life, not bothered about the damage he is doing to lives. The older one is a Lebanese business man who has been in the drug business for over two decades but has other business in the city of Kano. They wrap up their goods and walk through the main gate unquestioned by the fierce looking security guards. Ahmed notices as he peers through the darkness and thought within himself that he could just walk out of the gate like these two men although he doesn't know what has brought them into the vast compound. He concludes that he needs to monitor the gate very well to understand the process of exit.

The next day is very windy. There is an intense suicide bombing practice in progress as the supreme leader of the revolution is driven in an expensive hummer jeep into the camp. As he alighted, the practice came to an immediate halt with a loud shout coming from the camp commander. At once, everybody salute. They have been trained on how to pay obeisance to the self-styled supreme leader of the revolution. Many have lost their lives for failing to be prompt in paying the obeisance. Ahmed gets more confused and troubled by the day as the revelation of the inglorious lifestyle of these so called religious leaders come to light. Why should a person be killed for not paying obeisance to a mere man? If God whom they claim they are fighting for, decides to kill everybody who do not worship Him, how many people will be left in the world? *'The lifestyle of these religious fanatics is an indication that the struggle is selfish and personal,'* Ahmed thought to himself. His thought was abruptly cut short by another shout from the supreme commander signaling that the supreme leader of the revolution is about to make a speech to the trainees. The speech is a very brief and straight to the point one that aims to arouse their feelings and high their morale.

'The struggle continues. All the infidels must die! Big no to Western education. Big no to female education! We are sacrificing our lives for the struggle.

Of course you understand what I mean by that. When you die for the cause of Almighty Allah, you are sure of very rich and good rewards. Therefore we are preparing you to exit this wicked world honorably. When we die, we go to God. But when they die, they go to the devil their father. Do not be afraid to die, death is a necessary end for all mortals always remember.'

The supreme leader concluded his speech without any formality and walked away briskly. The commander runs after him towards his waiting vehicle.

Ahmed whispered to his friend Alhassan,

'If this man believes in what he is saying, why are his children not here? They are in good universities in rich countries like Saudi Arabia, Jordan and Iran, and even his female children too ooo while he brings the children of the less privileged and the deceived here to be trained as merchant of death and destruction.'

═══➤•◦•◄═══

Later that evening, Ahmed goes to the security gate with an intention to see how permeable the security can be. He pretends to join them in their evening prayers. Initially, the security personnel used to pray separately from the others but in recent times the rules have been relaxed thus allowing other non-security people to join in the prayers. The prayer is longer than the usual prayers because the Imam, on rare occasion like this, spends time to preach on loyalty and to remind the security of their roles in the whole camp. After the prayer section, the security guards headed to their different security post. The chief security officer calls Ahmed to meet him where he is standing at the other side of the security post. Yaro, as he is popularly called, has been in the secret service for years. He whistles and sizes up Ahmed as he walks to him.

'May I offer you a cup of tea or water?' asked the chief security officer.

'Tea,' replied Ahmed cautiously.

He is aware of who is talking with him. He must remain composed to avoid any suspicion. If he said he wanted nothing, it will give room for more suspicion.

'Why tea?'

'I have preference for tea. And I need something very warm too.'

'Ahah, talking about something warm, why did you come out in the cold to pray with us while your mates prayed in the mosque inside?'

'Just to experience the coldness of tonight with you. And I can see other guys coming out here to pray sometimes.'

In few minutes the tea was served in small cups. Ahmed eagerly sips his tea but becomes dissatisfied at once. It has too much sugar but little milk.

Ahmed doesn't want any moment of silence. He searches his mind quickly on what to say.

'Why is there much sugar in the tea, uncle? Are you not afraid of diabetics?' he asked the observant Chief security officer.

'You never stop amusing me, boy. Before you have

diabetics, don't you know you must have either been dead by reason of your activities of suicide bombing or any other espionage activities in the cause of our jihad against the infidels? We don't intend to keep you people here for more than three years. The maximum year someone can stay here is three years. All of you are brought here for a temporary and urgent assignment. You need to prepare for paradise so forget about what you take into your stomach. I will even prefer every of you should have diabetics so that you will be propelled to carry out the suicide mission.'

'That is very correct.' retorted Ahmed.

He knows very well that he has to play along. Perhaps the chief security officer's statement could be a test on his loyalty. He thought to himself, having understood the implication of being suspected of disloyalty as exemplified in the case of other victims who were used as demonstration for suicide bombing.

'I am happy that you understand the mission here. I will like you to work with the intelligence service.'

'Me?' replied Ahmed.

'Yes, you,' he said drawing close to him, 'All you need to do is to listen to what all other people are saying in the camp and bring the report to me directly.'

'Okay Sir. I can do it very well,' he said with feigned excitement. This assignment will make my escape very easy, he thought.

'A very intelligent boy, I see,' the chief security officer nodded with approval.

When he indicated that he was going to join his

colleagues in training, the chief security officer waved him back to his seat and said in a cold hard voice,

'Do not be in a hurry to go. I have an urgent assignment for you. I have taken care of your training parade, your absence is pardoned.'

When did this man contact the commander about my absence from training? Ahmed thought, surprise written all over his face. They have been together in the past few hours and he had not seen him put a call through to anyone or even answered a call. He looked at the security officer, 'Sir you must be supernatural.'

'Why did you say so? Only Almighty Allah is supernatural,' replied the chief security officer.

'I was wondering how you communicated with the commander that I would be absent from the training today without making a phone call or sending someone or going there,' queried Ahmed.

The chief security officer laughed softly and said,

'Do you know you can communicate without talking or seeing somebody? Do you know that in this camp there are people watching you and others every minute? Your activities are monitored and relayed immediately to the commander and me. That was how I was able to locate you my boy. We found out you are always alone meditating and this shows that you are intellectual. It's people like you we need in the secret service.'

Ahmed was stupefied, thanking his stars he has not taken any foolish steps.

'But why are these observers not visible?' he asked.

The security officer guffawed for some time until he finally responded,

'Who said they are not visible? Of course they eat with you, play with you and even talk with you. Now from this moment you are one of them. Your assignment is to monitor everybody no matter how highly placed he may be. When people are talking, eavesdrop. We need to pin the disloyal people down and nail them.'

The word 'eavesdrop' rang a bell on Ahmed's heart. He remembered when he was talking to Alhassan by the trees and saw some people watching them from afar. *They must be part of the secret service. Spies,* he concluded in his mind.

Ahmed was about to go away to meet the other people when he slipped by the edge of the step and fell with his thumb caught in between the iron bar on the protector. He looked at his thumb and could hardly see any sign of the cut. No redness too. He pressed thumb at the spot of the cut to see if it was a sore but saw it wasn't it. He quietly stood up and walked towards his collogues, with the chief security officer not showing any sympathy, or at least not showing any emotion.

Ahmed muttered,

'These guys are really heartless and wicked. Do they even have feelings for their children at all?'

The training for the day was concluded in a very short time and the trainees were dispatched. There was an urgent assignment that day. The terrorist were planning to bomb a night club in the city center and they have picked two of the older trainees to carry out the assignment. The training was ended early so that the masters would concentrate on the two guys who were assigned for the assignment. Ahmed monitored the movement of the two guys chosen for this assignment to see if they would be escorted and by how many people. If there is none, then escape will not be as difficult as he has thought it would be. All he needed to do was to pretend to be ready for an operation. On a second thought he remembered that one do not choose when one is ready for an assignment. The camp commander makes the choice. He noticed some strange men came into the camp to pick the guys. *But what happens at the sight of the bombing? When do those escort back out?* These are questions he need to find urgent answers to if his escape must be successful.

Ahmed and Alhassan met during lunch at the make shift cafeteria the next day. It was a sad afternoon. Apart from the fact that the food was scrappy and cold, the cafeteria was littered with crumbs of bread, rice and pieces of meat because most of the campers avoid eating them. These days, the nutrients of the foods have been deliberately decreased. No more chicken, steaks, soft drinks, no more chili cheese fries covered in chopped onions and even the atmosphere of the restaurant has been cold and unwelcoming.

'What are we going to do?' Sadam Alhasan moaned as they slid into their seat covered at the sides.

'We need to take our destinies in our hand,' Ahmed said with a sigh.

'I don't know how you can still be referring to your

escape plan when you are being closely monitored and watched,' Sadam Alhassan refused to deceive himself to believing that escape is possible from this hell.

'We heard you were with the chief security officer for a long time facing interrogation yesterday. I feel it is a risk to be seen with you for fear of being seen a compliance.'

'By people or by you?' Ahmed looked up at his friend.

'By me,' Alhassan replied slowly with his brow raised.

'Who told you that rubbish? My discussion with the chief security officer is a talk that will even help our escaping possible.'

'Which escape?' retorted Sadam Alhassan. 'If you are caught and killed, I will deny ever knowing you or what you are up to.'

'Now listen to me, Alhassan. If you stay back here your death is a matter of time, if you escape and you are caught, your death is immediate but if you escape and you succeed, your death will come for you in old age and you will surely save more people from getting into the trap of these evil ones,' Ahmed told Alhassan calmly like a preacher who was trying to persuade his members to pay their tithe.

They managed to eat the food even though it was not good enough for even a dog. It is very dangerous to stay hungry in the camp because of the rigorous training. If one faints during training or shows any sign of weakness, one will be used as a training material for suicide operation within the camp. With this is mind, most of the potential suicide bombers are forced to eat anything to remain strong enough for the training exercise.

Ahmed made up his mind not to discuss the escape plan with Sadam Alhassan any longer for fear that he might leak out the secret out of cowardice. He quickly changed the topic while they ate.

Other people came into the cafeteria and they did not show any sign of resentment about the food any longer. Many of them were excited while the rest were indifferent. A particular group were however expressionless. You could not tell if they were happy or sad. They just walked into the cafeteria, took their food, eat faster than anybody and walked out like ghosts. These were the set of people that are already aware they would be used for the next operation outside the camp because they have completed the full training. Hence, they await opportunity for targets to be available.

As soon as they have eaten enough to replenish their appetite, Alhasan asked, 'What deal do you have with the chief security officer?'

'It is a secret,' Ahmed responded sharply.

Alhassam waited for a short while and said, 'Come on. What are you hiding from me? I believe we are pals and we are in this together.'

'Trust me, the information does not concern you,' Ahmed paused indecisively before he continued, 'You need to be careful. I mean very careful. Do not talk to anybody even if you think the person is your friend. In this camp, there are no friends but fellow canons. If you take my advice seriously, you will be safe in this camp and if you are lucky, your escape will work out well. I warn you, never discuss our escape plan with anybody. It is more complicated than you think. Nobody has ever planned an escape from here since this camp was created. We will be the first to be doing this, and after us I do not think there will be another because it is either the camp would be destroyed or there will be no room for any camper to think of it because our escape will teach the administrators a bitter lesson.'

Alhassan let the spoon he was holding fall into the bowl he was eating from and stared for several seconds at the dirty table in front of him. Every ounce of hope for the future drained out of him in the few minutes he has been talking with Ahmed. He did not even have the strength to ask him why he had to tell him all this and how they got to this stage of despondency.

There was a long silence. An awkward one.

Ahmed cleared his throat and said, 'We know the Holy Koran doesn't favour the shedding of innocent blood or the wanton destruction of life and property. There is a great doubt if our religious leader read the Holy Koran or the great religious books by our sages at all. I have read the Holy Koran severally. My mentor, the late Emir taught me the tenants of the Islamic religion and all points to the fact that the religion is all about peace, peace and peace. That is why I must do everything to escape this satanic camp.'

'Oh my God!' Alhassan managed to exclaim weakly.

'So many Muslims, especially the educated ones, do not support all this violence being done in the name of God, the most merciful and the most beneficial. If you read the book written by Dr. Alberka Mohammed, you will understand what I am saying. Do you know him?'

'No.'

'He is a former lecturer in the City University in the capital. He traveled to Europe where he is trying to enlighten the world on the truth about our religion. He told the world that Islam has nothing to do with killing, mutilating, bombing and so on.'

'Does he have backing from other wealthy Islamic country?' Alhassan asked.

'I thought of that, too. No, he doesn't. And there is no way they will back him up openly because these wealthy countries need to balance the interest of their business with the mentality of this uninformed people.'

'I don't care which interest they are trying to balance but the Holy Book enjoins us to say the truth all the times and not to consider material gains. This is crazy. Why will our leaders be doing this to us?' Alhassan asked, desperation and hurt creeping into his voice.

'I don't know. What I know is that I am a Muslim. My father was a Muslim before he died. My mother is still practicing Islamic. Saddam my brother, also. But I don't understand why most of our Islamic leaders are being cruel and inhumane.'

'This suicide mission is totally nonsense. Surprisingly, none of these terrorist and religious fanatics leaders' children ever go on suicide mission.

I have never heard of any of them going on suicide mission but they use innocent people as loose cannons. What are the conditions precedent to be qualified as a suicide bomber?' Alhassam retorted.

'I was hoping the chief security officer might shed some light on it. We discussed almost everything but he did not justify the reason why a person will take pleasure in causing pain to other people in the name of religion. These people have so degenerated our religion to the extent that a very large number of them are usually devotees at the altar of mammon or ill-gotten wealth mainly gotten from selling hard drugs like cocaine and heroin or on the other hand they dedicate considerable amount of time stealing their nations wealth and storing them in banks belonging to the people they call infidels. Inordinate power, opulence, terrible and rapacious greed powered by selfish interest.'

Alhassan quietly picked his spoon from the plate and placed it into his pocket, and stood up with his head bowed. 'Ahmed, let's get out of here before I lose my mind,' he said almost to himself.

Ahmed stood up from the table and walked towards Alhassan. With compassion, he said, 'I am sorry. You know we are in this together. Since I am now close to the chief security officer, I can exercise as much leeway as possible to find respite for you and me. There are several ways to get out of this hell. I am going to consider each way very critically before I discuss with you in a safe place where there will be no prying ears.'

'I understand. But the handwriting on the wall is

very clear. There are dangers ahead," Alhassan said bitterly. 'Being on the receiving end of knowing that one day, in fact very soon, you will be used as a suicide bomber to kill people who have done nothing to you is very painful. No wonder the suicide bombers are always drugged before they execute the heinous act.'

Ahmed swallowed hard, 'I can't blame you for how you feel because I feel the same way too. But the difference between us is simply that you are hesitating to act failing to realize that either way you go, death is inevitable. Why not choose the better of the two options which will lead you to a life-time peace.'

Going down the step outside the cafeteria, Alhassan quickly walked past Ahmed to his hostel. He looked down at his shirt, it was stained with the food they just ate. He fell straight on the mat in the room he shared with ten other boys. He stretched his hand, switched on the standing fan to the highest, and closed his eyes.

It was much sunny in the Sambisa forest later that afternoon. The temperature was 43 degree Celsius. The sun was so scourging that people in the camp even heaviness of the sun was so much felt that the campers could not hide their discomfort. Many of them reached out for the shades of the trees and flowers to escape the scourging sun. Ahmed, on a dirty jeans shirt and pants, moved slowly towards the security gate to survey and consolidate his escape plot under the guise of visiting the chief security officer.

It was just before twelve when the chief security

officer walked up to where Ahmed was standing near the security office operation base. His chauffeur drew in beside the checkpoint and as he switched off the engine, the door opened and Ahmed climbed into the rear seat.

'You had better not be wearing dirty cloths like this. It gives the impression that you are troubled about what God has destined for you,' the chief security officer said.

Ahmed smiled pretending to be in sync with the statement. But inwardly, those words were like hot red coal in an open wound. The disdain he has for the activities in this evil camp increased drastically and his resolve to escape was now heightened by chief security officer's statement. *Who are these unworthy mortals to determine what God has destined for anyone?'* he thought to himself. He reached out his hand and closed the door of the car.

'Sir, I am on a dirty cloth because we just finished some training and I didn't bother to change before coming here.'

'Yeah, I monitored your practice. You seem in very good form and I like your enthusiasm tonight,' the chief security said, nodding in admiration.

'Why shouldn't I be? I believe in the struggle and I want to play an important part too,' he said to make the chief security officer believe he was immersed in the struggle.

'I hope you have not told anybody of your new assignment? Especially your friend Alhassan. We have received the report of your very close relationship with him these days. However, my trust for you do not dwindle.'

Ahmed has learned very fast how security chiefs pretend to trust someone but are only setting them up. His instinct has told him not to trust anybody on this camp. He quickly replied, 'No. Of course not.'

'Excellent!' exclaimed the chief security officer. 'I wouldn't like anything to spoil our relationship because it is obvious now that I have taken you as my son. Now let's go to my office. Let me tell you about an assignment I have for you.'

As they were talking, a group of sober people were brought into the camp. They were kidnapped victims, and majority of them were girls. In the camp, there are two groups of people. Those who were forcefully brought in by the bandits and those, like Ahmed, whose families forced them to go into the camp.

The chief security officer opened the door of the office. A guard came in and poured some hot coffee from a pot for him.

The chief security officer tapped his finger in enthusiasm, 'Black coffee? I like black coffee. It makes your brain sharp.'

The guard placed the steaming pot on the table and reached into his pocket. He brought out a wrapped item from his pocket and handed it over to the chief security. Mohamed Mambo is the name of the guard but he was nicknamed Pabloo Escobar because he knew all the drug joints within and outside the vicinity. What he handed the chief security officer is the best quality of crack cocaine. It has been established that all the top echelon of the camp are drug addicts and the camp is funded from drug money.

'Is this the best?' he asked the guard.

'Yes Sir. I got it from mail. It is perfect.'

'Shut your dirty mouth!' shouted the chief security officer. 'Nothing is ever perfect in this life, you should have known that already. That is why despite my strong adherence to our great religion, I still find myself breaking the rules like this stuff you handed me.'

As they were still talking, the door flung open and the camp commandant came in with two ladies covered with hijab such that you could hardly see their eyeballs. As the ladies entered the office, they quickly threw away their coverings as though they were a burden. They looked very seductive in their almost nude state. The ladies were professional prostitutes but who pretended to be genuine Muslims to the outside world to avoid a backlash from the genuine devotees. This type of visit by ladies of easy virtue is a regular occurrence for the chief security officer and the camp commandant. The camp commandant looked at the chief security officer and said,

'I promised you some electrifying girls. Here they are. These ones are voluptuously beautiful so eat and have your fill. You can start your paradise from here. And mind you, these particular ones are special order from across the border, specially selected for you.'

'Thank you very much. You are right anyway. I

salivated on just seeing them,' the chief security officer replied with zest.

He took a glance at Ahmed and signaled to him to wait outside the office while he and the camp commandant settled down to satisfy their sexual urge.

Ahmed was shocked and confused. This was a contradiction of what he had been taught as a Muslim. The religion is totally against any form of immorality and abhors prostitution. What are these people standing for? What do they represent? Are they truly fighting for God or they have their own self-serving agenda? Trying to resolve these questions, increased the possibility for his escape. It's been three hours he waited outside the office yet there wasn't any indication that they would soon be done. The funny sounds coming from the locked room kept on increasing and becoming very loud and irritating. The indifference shown by the security guards around showed that they were no strangers to this type of sound and groaning.

After many hours, the camp commandant and the chief security officer came out of the office sweating profusely. They walked pass Ahmed who was sitting on the chair outside the office. The two girls did not come out. Few minutes later, six hefty men carrying two big empty sacks walked into the office and in less than ten minutes they were coming out of the office with full sacks. The objects in the sack had the shape of a human being. Different thought ran through Ahmed's mind. However, having been warned earlier by one of the guards not to ask too many question as it will be very dangerous to his continual survival in the camp, he kept mute. Later, the duo walked back to the office, this time wearing a different outfit. The chief security officer signaled to Ahmed to come into the office. Two minutes later, two other boys joined them in the office. Ahmed had been seeing the two boys in the camp and he was aware that one of them was due for suicide bombing assignment. His heart skipped a beat for fear that his plot to escape had been uncovered.

'The three of you will be going for an urgent assignment in the city center,' the chief security officer finally said after many minutes of silence. 'Specifically the motor park,' he continued, 'we must do the work of God by eliminating the infidels from our land. They will be coming to the motor park today. One of you would be dressed with the bombs while the other two would pretend to be passengers. Three of you must not behave as if you know one another. The assignment of two of you will be to survey the vicinity and identify where we can do the most damage on lives and property,'

Ahmed noticed that the chief security officer was avoiding eye contact with him. *This is callous*, he thought to himself. These are Satan's messengers, he concluded. Happily, he would use this opportunity to escape even if the lot falls on him to carry the bomb.

The chief security shouted, 'Now, the three of you get out and wait for the next instruction. We are about to make a big statement to the infidels. Stay outside and wait for the executioners to ferry you down to the site of operation.'

Ahmed and the other two guys walked out of the office and were taken to another section of the camp where they were given some white substance which Ahmed suspected to be hard drugs. While the other two took theirs immediately, Ahmed made sure no one was watching him, flung his own away and pretended to have taken it. The executioner was surprised at the speed of Ahmed's consumption and hailed him. In forty five minutes they were done and set to proceed on the evil assignment.

The parcel of bomb was neatly wrapped in the inner jacket of one of them while Ahmed and the second boy will attract the crowd to the boy wearing the explosives. The executioner lectured them thoroughly what was expected from them and reemphasized the reason they should pay the supreme sacrifice for the Almighty God. They left the camp in a Range Rover Jeep. Ahmed was not able to say the last goodbye to his friend and confidant Alhassan. He had made up his mind he was not going to die like a dog for any reason but he pretended to play along. He was the only one with a clear thought as he did not take the drug meanwhile the other two guys were excited and eager to carry out the assignment.

The Range Rover arrived the motor park in about two hours. The three boys disembarked while the executioner stayed back in the Range Rover watching them move into the motor park. Seconds turned into minutes. The executioner was waiting to hear the sound of explosion so that he could speed off, but there was no sound even as the minutes turned into hour. *What had gone wrong?* He thought within himself? Suddenly he saw the other guy attached with Ahmed running towards his vehicle with panic written all over his face. Meanwhile, in the camp, the camp operators all tuned to the state radio channel where the news would break out first. There was anxiety everywhere.

The boy got to the executioner and started exclaiming as he panted for air, 'Sir, Ahmed, Ahmed, Ahmed...'

'Eheh... What has happened to Ahmed? You are on operation boy! You talk or I cut off your dull head?' the executioner cut him short angrily.

'He disappeared as soon as we got into the motor park! He started running towards another direction. We were utterly confused because it was not part of our plan,' the boy said, still trying to comport himself from shaking.

'I thought as much. I knew that that bastard will betray us!' the executioner exclaimed in annoyance.

Before he could conclude his statement, the bomb went off, he quickly asked the other guy to get into the car and then they sped off.

'This is a bad one!' he shouted. 'I warned the commandant about that boy,' he continued bitterly, 'that guy called Ahmed looks too smart for his age. I noticed the drug did not have any effect on him. At the moment we need to speed off very fast for security purpose. You understand me?'

'Yesss Sir.'

The commotion caused by the bombing was severe.

The police and the emergency services immediately came to the site and started evacuating the victims of the explosion to near-by government hospital.

Ahmed sneaked into a restaurant in the motor park far away from the site of the explosion. It was the first time he was seeing such pandemonium and panic in a long while now. The major delicacy of this restaurant is burger. The restaurant was particularly full because many people rushed into the place when the bomb went up and the police have curtailed movement as a security measure. Sniff dogs and anti-bomb experts were everywhere to see if there were other bombs yet to explode. Ahmed sat in a corner watching everybody. On his table was a burger and some half-drunk bottles of Coca-Cola a customer abandoned halfway when the bomb went off. The security men walked into the restaurant sizing up everybody inside. As the security tried to observe the people inside the restaurant, a tall athletic man walked in and pointed towards Ahmed. The police and their dogs walked to Ahmed's table looking sternly at him. One of them asked,

'Why were you running when you walked into the park?'

Ahmed looked at him straight in the eyes and replied, 'I was pressed so I had to run to ease myself.'

This was part of the training he received in the camp. They have been taught not to get intimidated by the looks of any security agent. They were told that eye to eye contact is an indication of innocence. The security agents walked away with the dogs while Ahmed heaved a sigh of relieve. Like a hungry lion, he settled himself to the burger and the already opened coke on his table. Many people looked at him in astonishment. By this time, the security had cleared the place; all dead bodies removed and normal activities continued, although not as lively as before. Ahmed ate from table to table not minding people's questioning look. He didn't know where he would sleep for the night. He moved out of the mall and walked very fast in the opposite direction he came from the camp. He walked and looked around every now and then to see if anybody was following him from time to time. He was being cautious because he did not want to underestimate the capacity of the terrorist organization like the one he just escaped from. Not very far from where the restaurant was located, he cited a small mosque. He walked straight in and sat by a corner to pray. There were few other men praying although it wasn't the general praying hour. Ahmed took notice of a man who looked very familiar and as he was trying to put together where he had met him, the man stood up and walked out of the mosque. This must be a dangerous hide-out for me, he thought. As he became agitated, he stood up and walked out of the mosque. Outside, Ahmed saw the man on phone call and backing the door. He walked stealthily away and moved into the next street adjacent to the mosque from where he could see everything happening in and around the mosque. The man on the phone had already finished talking to the person on the other end and instead of going back into the mosque, he stood by the entrance gate looking around. Less than five minutes, a jeep stopped at the entrance of the mosque and the chief security officer of the camp stepped out looking terribly angry. Ahmed could see them from the vantage point but they could not see him. Both men walked into the mosque but in few minutes they were out again looking frantically at all directions. At once, Ahmed remembered where he had first seen the man. He was the one who had forced him into the camp on the first day. He turned around and started moving into the cronies where vehicles could not enter. He knew he had to move very far from these evil men and very fast too. If it happened the second time, he might not be as lucky as this again.

It was night. Ahmed had walked a very long distance from the mosque. Tired and worn out, he saw a house with an elderly man standing outside there. He walked straight to the man and asked him for water. The old man obliged and even gave him a little water to wash his feet. He offered him a place to rest for the night with a stern warning that he could not accommodate him beyond breakfast the next day. While Ahmed had rested for some hours, the elderly man walked to the sitting room where he was sitting staring at nothing in particular.

'Who are you running from?' asked the elderly man thoughtfully.

He slowly walked across the sitting room towards the window. For a long time he stood there looking at the dim light from the bulb of the street light and the passing beams of vehicles. Ahmed could see the furnishing of the sitting room more clearly now. Some pictures of great men and heroes hung on the wall; Malcolm X, martin Luther king and Nelson Mandela. There was a very big table with some Arabic inscriptions and the chairs were carved from big mahogany wood. A wash hand basin hung on the wall with a towel stand. The elderly man waited patiently for Ahmed to answer but when Ahmed remained silent, he turned to him and asked,

'Where are you coming from and where are you going to?'

'You look like one running from danger. Boy, the times are rough. You need to be guided.'

Ahmed, still trying to think if he could trust the man said, 'Sir, the story of my life is encapsulated in tears and pain.'

The elderly man replied," I am not asking you for the story of your life. Truly, some people have life very good while others have life very bad for them. What I want to know from you is simple. Who are you running from? Tell me the truth so that I know how to help you.'

Ahmed decided to take the risk of trusting the man, 'I escaped from the terrorist camp in Sambisa forest.'

The elderly man looked at him with a quiet smile on his face and said, 'I know. Almighty Allah wants you to live. My son was kidnapped by them, I do not know if he is still alive.'

'What is his name and how does he look?' asked

Ahmed, trying to see if he could help to provide the man with vital information about his son.

'His name is Alhassan, lanky........

Ahmed interrupted on hearing the name, 'He was my only friend in the camp. Two of us were planning this escape together but unfortunately we were taken unaware.'

'How do you mean?' replied the elderly man who was now eager to hear more about his son.

'Few weeks before we were to escape, I was given an assignment to blow up the motor park on a suicide mission so in the process, I escaped,' Ahmed said looking into the big mirror in the sitting room.

'Alhassan my only son, I pray ALAAH protects you and give you courage to do the right thing,' the elderly man said hysterically, talking to no one in particular. There was a very long and cold silence after this. Then he coughed vigorously. Ahmed rushed to give him some water but the elderly man said,

'My son, please do not bother. I was once a victim of those wicked people,' he began to say. 'I tried to resist them from taking my son, Alhassan but they did not like my effrontery, so they beat me until I had internal injuries. They left me to die but the Almighty Allah saved me. Ever since these extremists started operating in this country, they have been visiting everybody with wickedness. The whole country is living under the bone −cracking weight of the wickedness of these people. You don't have to look too far to behold the manifestation of the desperate wickedness that lies in the heart of these people who claim to be fighting for the Almighty Allah. Everywhere you turned to in this city, there is bombing, murder, kidnapping, raping and stealing, all in the name of God. I am tired and fed up!' he shouted.

Ahmed stared at him. He looked like a man who was losing his sanity. Ahmed felt bad he could not comfort the elderly man. The elderly man beckoned to Ahmed and said,

'Come very close to me, my son. I would like to tell you the story of my life. Would like to do that very urgently.'

'Okay Papa,' said Ahmed.

Quickly he took a piece of paper and a biro from the table near the large mirror.

'No, no,' the elderly man shook his head vehemently, 'That paper will waste our time. I am running out of time. I have a small tape recorder in my room. Quickly get it. My room is the second door from here and you will find the tape recorder on the bedside table.' As Ahmed moved towards the room, the sound of an explosion was heard afar off, he stopped abruptly and looked at the elderly man, who signaled to him to continue. It was not difficult locating the tape recorder; he picked it and rushed back to the sitting room. He removed the small tape recorder from the leather cover, making a check of the cassette and the batteries.

'I am really anxious to hear this story,' Ahmed said replacing the cassette.

'Are you ready?' asked the elderly man.

'Yes, Papa'

'Then sit down and listen attentively. I am going to turn off the light for security reasons and make the place more comfortable for the talk.'

'Which security reasons?' Ahmed asked.

'The secret agents are always on the ploy. If your lights are not off at this ungodly hours they believe you are up to something.' The elderly man stretched his hand and switched off the lights but left the table dim lamb on.

The elderly man started to narrate his life story in a very sorrowful tone, interrupted constantly by his dip cough. They were interrupted by a very loud bang outside the house near the roadside and next was exchange of bullets between two trucks. A stray bullet pierced through the window and hit the elderly man at the back of his head. At once, he slumped on the floor.

'*Awusubilahi!*' Ahmed exclaimed in terror, staring at the lifeless body and watched as blood dribbling from the torso drew zigzag on the dirty tiles on the floor. His fingers danced backwards on the table. '*Ya Allah,*' he whispered, gasping.

The elderly man's face was like a statue. His two brilliant eyes looked at Ahmed intently like flames in a skull. Ahmed shuddered, lifting his hand as if to shield himself from a powerful light. His eyes moved slowly over the body that laid on the floor. Suddenly, Ahmed saw the elderly man smiled almost wistfully, and the blood dropping from the gun shot increased tremendously. Sweaty substance gushed from his face like bubbles. *Am I dreaming?* Ahmed exclaimed.

'My son,' the old man said faintly. Ahmed gasped, a sound letting from his throat. 'Papa? Did I hear you speak?' he asked with hot tears flowing down his cheek.

'Son, I have very little time left. Check under the bed in my room, I left some money there. Take it and run to safety. Do not forget to tell the whole world our story if you finally make it to safety. I have a grave behind this house... bury me there. If ever you see Alhassan again, ahhh...my body aches...my chest...' the elderly man groaned in pain. Ahmed knelt soberly by the man, not minding that the knee part of his trouser robbed the blood on the floor. The man continued, 'Tell him I love himmmmmm,' he managed to say. He took a deep breath and his eyes slowly closed.

Ahmed caressed the elderly man's face. He struggled to carry the body outside through the back door. To his surprise, he saw the grave neatly dug. *The old man had really prepared for his death,* he thought. He had not done a funeral before but he remembered how his father was buried. He became troubled by the absence of an Imam to pray for the deceased's fridaus. However, he knew he had to bury the body as fast as possible as instructed by the elderly man himself. He proceeded to say the prayers as best as he could, buried the elderly man and made a bold inscription on a board, *'Here lies the body of one of the most holy men I have met in my entire life,'* and placed it gently on the grave. He went into the house, cleaned the blood stained floor and arranged the house properly. He sat on the sofa to have a little rest but as nature cannot be cheated, he dozed off unintentionally.

Ahmed was rudely awakened by the loud sound of a vehicle moving in front of the house. He peered through the window and to his utmost surprise, the morning is far gone. The movement of people in the vicinity was pugnacious and the incessant noise from the market filled the air. Even a visitor, without anyone telling him, can easily detect the state of insecurity in the community. Here, violence gives no notice. He went straight into the bedroom, checked under the bed and found the money wrapped in a black bag. He carefully brought it out and counted them before replacing them back into the bag. The words of the elderly man kept ringing on his ears, *'Run to safety.'* Now with this money he could run to safety and tell the whole world about the camp, the Sambisa forest. He took a bigger bag and sit the money in it. He meticulously checked himself. He almost slapped himself when he saw his blood stained trouser. *Ahmed, if you had gone outside with this bloodstained trouser, I wouldn't have forgiven you, anyway,* he told himself. He looked around and saw some winter clothes and two pairs of trousers. The trousers were exactly his size. He thought they must be Alhassan's. Happily, he threw himself in one. The winter clothes, majorly sweaters and hoodie, were bigger than him, but he did not care. Quickly, he stuffed them and the second trouser into the bigger bag, leaving his own trouser carelessly on the floor. As he walked towards the toilet, the urge to clean up and look nice sprang up within him. He thought it would reduce any form of suspicion from people. He rushed into the shower. After a while, he checked himself in the mirror and was satisfied with how refreshing he looked after the quick bath. Through the mirror, his eyes saw a hung bag partly covered by a water heater. He put down the bag and was about to search through it when a blast was heard outside the house again, People started running in different directions. Ahmed withdrew his hand from the bag, dashed behind the bathroom door and hid himself. The commotion continued outside the house unabated. There was exchange of gun fire and bullets flew freely. People fell and many soaked in the pool of blood. The scene could best be described as extravagant anarchy. This wasn't a strange occurrence in the community as it had become part and parcel of the entire inhabitants of the city. Suddenly, a rude knock was heard on the door. Ahmed's heart banged. Sweat began to form on his brow as he cleaved to the wall of the back door he was hiding. The knock persisted. He managed to tiptoe to the corner where he kept the bag containing the money, picked it and hid it under the bed while he sat on the bed as the knock became more intensified. After a while, the knock seized. Ahmed peeped to see if the person knocking had gone. He could hear some loud voices. One of them sounded familiar. *The camp commandant!* Ahmed muttered. Then the elderly man's voice reverberated again, *'Take the money and run to safety.'* Like a flush of water, many things started hovering in his mind. *Thank God the doors are bullet proof,* he thought. He was not going to open that door even if the knock continued for years but he knew he had to act very fast now as his enemies were closer than he thought.

'What on earth are they looking for in this place? Or had Alhassan spoken something? I will never fall a victim of these evil men a second time,' he mumbled as the thought of the camp made him shiver in terror. Cautiously, he tiptoed into the bathroom where he could have a proper view of what was going on outside. He saw the commander of the camp pacing up and down, looking very anxious. There was a last knock, this time harder. Then gun fires ranted the air. Now it was the police. The commander scrammed to safety. The police came and tried their hands on the door handle and found it locked. They soon entered their van and drove away. Immediately, the commander crept out from the drainage channel where he was hiding. He had just managed to escape from the police. He had been on the wanted list for years and somehow he always made himself invincible. Ahmed could see the commander from where he was standing. His car was now damaged by the small powerful shots of the police. He hit the car with his leg in annoyance as it downed on him that it was now useless until it was repaired. Quickly, he crossed the road and moved as fast as his legs could take him and disappeared into the thin air. Ahmed didn't see the others that followed him again.

He put his hand up in praises to God and quickly went back to search the bag he was fumbling with before the banging of the door. *'A pistol?'* Quickly, he zipped off a side pocket in the corner of the bag, *'Life bullets and another authentic gun? Oh...Allah...Allah!'* He stared at it for some times and then an idea pumped up in his mind. Yes, he must take them and use them to run to safety. He had become a man overnight. He reminded himself of a song he once heard, 'Sometimes you gonna fight to be a man.' He neatly put the long gun into his bag and put the pistol inside the dip pocket of the trouser he was wearing and covered it with his big shirt. He felt a strong confidence come upon him as he moved towards the door. He turned around and waved a final goodbye to the picture of the elderly man on the wall and said,

'When I run to freedom, I will reward your kindness by fighting for the release of your son and my friend Alhassan. I pray he is alive by that time. Amin.'

He unlocked the door, walked out boldly, locked the door again, and threw the keys into his bag. Although he had no particular place to go, he confidently walked down the street, He kept walking until he waved to a cab.

'Along,' Ahmed was surprise by the sudden change of his voice. It sounded more mature.

The cab slowed down and he jumped at the back seat. After some minutes of driving, the driver looked back and said,

'Young man, where are you dropping?'

'Keep going, I tell you when I get there.'

'Hey listen, I want to branch off before the police check point down the road,' replied the driver.

'Police check point?' retorted Ahmed. He didn't even think twice on what the driver had said. His ears might have not heard *before* but heard clearly *police check point*. 'Okay. I will drop in front of the big hotel up there then,' he said pointing to the building ahead of them.

He alighted from the vehicle and as he turned, he spotted a rest inn created by the five star hotel on the other side. He settled for it as a safer place to hide while he strategized on his next line of action. In deep thought, Ahmed stood in front of the rest inn. He could see a troubled city from the rubbles of a destroyed country and stunning abilities of her people to the betrayal of wicked religious leaders. His search for peace must take him out of this country to a far land, very far from the terrorist bombs he had known all his life. Ahmed, realizing he was standing too long in that position, moved straight to the reception. He smiled partly as he remembered the first time he entered a hotel. He was a child then. He followed his parents to Saudi Arabia for a religious festival. However this time, he was alone. He booked for a small room and left a tip for the receptionist who was from the same locality with him. As he gave Ahmed the forms to fill, he asked,

'Are you alone?'

'Yes. Why?' Ahmed asked curiously.

'Just considering your age. One would have thought you are with somebody.'

"Have I told you my age?' retorted Ahmed.

'Your face reveals your age,' replied the receptionist with a smile.

''How old do you think I am? Ahmed inquired further.

'Maximum, eighteen years.'

'I will be twenty-three in two months,' replied Ahmed knowing the risk of telling his true age. Most hotels do not accommodate teens in this part of the world, even if you are eighteen.

''I am surprised. You look very young for your age.'

'Thank you,' replied Ahmed. 'It is because I take good care of myself.'

The receptionist looked at him carefully and said, 'If you have good money, you will take good care of yourself.'

Ahmed hesitated but he needed to get the receptionist off his back. He saw the lips of the receptionist was burnt due to excessive smoking. He smiled sheepishly and replied,

'You do not need good money to stop the dirty habit of smoking.'

The receptionist did not find it funny. He looked at Ahmed sarcastically and kept quiet. He called one of the cleaners to carry Ahmed's bag and show him his room but Ahmed politely turned down the offer and walked briskly behind the cleaner. The cleaner led him to a very small room that looked stuffy and damp.

'Are there no better rooms?' asked Ahmed.

'The big rooms are twice the price of this one. And

since you are alone, just manage this room,' replied the cleaner as he walked out of the room.

———⟫•○•⟪———

AHMED SALIM sat on the bed looking at the ceiling and totally lost in taught about his poor mother. *'How will I see Mama without uncle knowing?'* he thought.

His mind flashed through the people he had met and all that he had passed through in life; the elderly man who gave him this life-line, Alhassan, the son and his own friend, his Imam, his father, his uncle, and poor traditional values of his tribe, the periods he spent in the camp and how he was to die as a suicide bomber without prior notice. Ahmed concluded that the chief security officer was nothing but a traitor. The period Ahmed stayed in the camp made him a tough man but it did not destroy his sense of justice. He became even physically fit because of the routine exercise and training. And more daring, inventive and he has the stamina to stand the test of time. He could now cope with any situation but the only challenge he had was the burden of the camp life. The activities and life in the militant training camp has altered the cause of his life exceedingly, the unbelievable savagery in the camp confirms the reality of the existence of Satan, 'But are those atrocities really the works of Satan?' he asked aloud like there was someone with him in the room.

There was a soft knock on door. It made him remember the hard knocks that came persistently on the elderly man's door. This knock was a direct opposite of it. *This knock is sweet. That was bitter*, he muttered as he peeped through the pin hole on the door. It was the receptionist. He opened the door slightly.

'I came to check if you need anything,' the receptionist said with almost closed lips, like one speaking through his nose.

'Thanks, there is a phone here. If I need anything, I will call you,' replied Ahmed softly but when he remembered that he had not eaten since morning, he quickly added,

'Please give me a soft drink and meat pie.'

'How many bottles of soft drink?' the receptionist asked.

Ahmed, getting really irritated, responded in a very sarcastic tone, 'How many people are in the room?'

'Sorry Sir. But some customers buy up to three bottles of coke at a time,' the receptionist's voice suddenly went sober.

'Okay, I need to rest now. Just let me have one bottle of *7 up* and one meat pie.'

'I'll be back in a minute with the items,' responded the receptionist as he sped off.

Ahmed went back to the bed, took off his shoes and waited patiently for the order. Thirty minutes passed and the order did not come. He stood up, locked the door, opened his bag and repeatedly counted the money. His mind went back to the suicide mission from where he escaped. Ahmed did not regard wanton violence and wickedness as the work of Satan. He believed it is the result of the evil inherent in the human nature and the main cause of this evil is their dark instinct and barbaric culture. Why suicide bombings? Why these cruelty against our fellow men? Why the rape and burning down of villages which rendered people homeless and creating orphans and widows. *In short, why is it that all these evil works ravaged throughout Nigeria today?* he muttered. Why do people sponsor such magnitude of evil with ill-gotten wealth mostly from drugs trade and official corruption? But what made him sober and annoyed the most is the hide under the cloak of religion. What has religion got to do with suicide bombing and mass murder? He was distracted by the hard knock on the door. He jumped up and peeped through the pinhole. It was the receptionist carrying a tray with the drink and meat pie. He opened the door half way. The look on his face sent a very clear message of disappointment which made the receptionist apologized at once. Ahmed, not wanting to waste any more time with the receptionist accepted the apologies in a rude hurry, collected the tray and paid the receptionist who hesitated a little before he left. Ahmed went back into the room and quietly ate the snacks and gulped the drink. The thought of the camp filled his mind again. While he was in the camp, he never met the main initiators of the activities and nobody ever made mention of them too. Even the elderly man did not even say anything about them. Does that mean they do not exist? Criminal bosses are skilled in hiding their true identity. In most cases, they operate through masqueraded agents who may never be traced to them. Newspaper headlines and major electronic media houses agog daily about suicide bombing, drug, dispute, prostitution rings and human trafficking to name a few. It is obvious that those arrested and paraded could not finance those activities themselves. Their initiators and sponsors are the religious extremists and some elites and political men in the country. Unfolding events have confirmed that these big time crime sponsors are real persons. They are powerful criminal king pin who have satanic conviction, who tend to accomplish their will through brain washing and righteous deception of the innocent puns. In fact, they keep transforming themselves into angels of light by pretending to be fighting the cause of the Almighty Allah. The satanic instinct of these sponsors could best be seen by the marks they leave behind to their executors. Many people find it difficult to decode the actions of these people. The uninformed rant the air with shots of *Allahuakbar*.

Ahmed was distracted again by a knock on the door. He pretended to be asleep but the knock came again, this time a little louder. He stood up and peeped through the main hole and found out that it was the receptionist again. He opened the door ajar in annoyance.

'What do you want?' Ahmed asked.

'I came to pick the bottle and to ask if you need any other thing,' the receptionist replied.

'You are disturbing me!' Ahmed yelled. 'If you want me to go to another hotel, please tell me. I have an intercom, if I need any other thing, I will let you know.

Am I the only guest in this hotel that you are dotting on me like this? Now come inside and take your bottle and tray.' The receptionist entered and took the bottle and tray.

'I am very sorry, Mister. I didn't mean to disturb you. I am only trying to show our hospitality in this hotel.'

'Thank you. Please do not suffocate me with your hospitality,' replied Ahmed.

'Okay Sir, if you need anything just call through the intercom and I will bring it in a second,' said the receptionist as he strolled away looking backward even as Ahmed entered the room and locked the door.

The day was already turning into night. The street lights were not as bright to give enough illumination to the streets. Ahmed opened the window in his room and looked through it. He could only see figures of people walking down the street but he could not see their faces. Men and women locked in each other's arm, cyclist moving at snail speed, cars roaring from the two directions blaring their horns and not minding the laws on noise pollution. Ahmed turned his gaze to the right, focusing on the three star hotel next to the rest inn he was staying. He noticed a truck. The truck looked very familiar. He looked intently again to be sure. Quickly, he dashed straight to the door of his room, opened it and rushed out. He was almost running out of the inn when it occurred to him that he did not lock his door. He returned, put some money in his pocket and hurriedly locked the door. He ran towards the vehicle and luckily for him nobody was in it. It was the vehicle that took him and the two boys to the motor park to blow it up. *Yes*, he thought to himself, they are at it again, they want to blow up this hotel with foreign tourist. He said aloud to himself, *'I need to act very fast.'*

He quickly turned towards the back gate of the hotel, knowing fully well that the assailants would strike through the front gate pretending to be guests.

'I dined with that devil. I can perceive the aroma of his wickedness around here,' he muttered, remembering his days in the terrorist camp and most recently the suicide attack he was supposed to execute in the mall. Ahmed got to the back gate. It was locked but a security officer was standing by it. 'No through fare, strictly for emergency' was boldly written on the gate. He beckoned at the security guard to come closer.

'What can I do for you?' the security officer shouted in a very harsh tone.

'There is an emergency you must attend to at once, Sir. You have suicide bombers in your hotel,' Ahmed blurted.

'Who told you? Are you trying to raise a hoax here?' asked the security guard as he corked his gun walking towards Ahmed.

'You need to act very fast. The black truck parked outside with the broken number plate is their vehicle, I know them very well. Any time they are going for such deadly mission they fix that number plate,' replied Ahmed, almost out of control.

The security guard immediately got the message

because he could remember that when the truck parked there, the broken number plate caught his attention and he had an intuition that this men were here for an evil mission. He suspected the broken number plate as a disguise but he did not think of suicide bombing. Hurriedly, he rushed to alert the central security. Alert was sent everywhere within the hotel premises. His mission accomplished, Ahmed slipped back into his rest inn. He quickly prepared for any emergency, packed his things neatly in the bag and positioned himself to a safe distance from the hotel in case the suicide mission succeeded. He positioned himself in a way that he would see people running up and down the hotel but nobody could see him. Within few seconds, the terrorist knew their cover had been blown. This time around, the camp commander was the leader of the mission. He had come with two boys; Alhassan and another boy. The commander, being a seasoned terrorist, managed to sneak out with the two boys, leaving the vehicle behind. While the security looked for them, they hid by the big flower garden. Ahmed saw the commander running away. This means any moment the two boys could detonate the bombs they were wearing. Ahmed moved quickly towards Alhassan and shouted,

'DON'T DO IT. Throw it off and run towards me now!".

Alhasssan turned immediately. It was Ahmed. Like a robot, he threw the bomb off and ran towards Ahmed. He had barely taken off when the other boy detonated his own and there was a loud explosion. However,

Alhassan managed to escape to safety. To Ahmed, this is a familiar ground. He took Alhassan to where he was hiding and monitoring every event unnoticed. As the flames from the fire caused by the explosion rose over the city, the sky became painted pink and orange. A heartbreaking view of the front view of the hotel and damaged vehicles can be likened to a tsunami or an active volcano. A constant plume of smoke rises from the site of the explosion and because it was night the plumes glowed red like a lava in the crater.

In Northeast of the country, this is almost an everyday occurrences. Human bodies are dismembered, littering the site of the incident. The last major suicide bombing was in a festival celebration ground. Many of the people lost their loved ones; people who managed to survive had to walk on dead bodies because the road was littered with human flesh and bones. The majority of the people, who are the real indigenes of the city are the opposite of the terrorists. They are lively people with soft and open hearts. They always welcome and protect strangers. The night has suddenly become sad, sorrowful and long. The police had already filled the site and condoning the whole place. Ahmed and Alhassan sneaked into the inn where Ahmed already had a room. Many guest had fled the Three Star Hotel to the rest inn Ahmed was staying. The lobby of the rest inn was filled with different people, many of the ladies wore a brightly coloured wrap skirts as if they planned it. The receptionist, as usual, was moving up and down looking confused and disorganized. He had not seen such number of guest at a time. Without saying a word, Ahmed and Alhasan walked past to Ahmed's room.

Until lately, few of the many puzzles the first time visitors to the city encounters could have been more intriguing than the notices in bold letters they find on the façade of many homes all around the city written in Arabic *Uninvited guest not wanted here*. If a visitor is not wanted in a particular place, he had to wander in his or her innocence. But why was attention drawn to uninvited guests? Are there special houses reserved for uninvited guest? Do people go to places uninvited for the fun of it? Surely nobody in his right senses will go to another person's house if not invited. Surely, any person who visited where he was not wanted dared not complain if they were roughened and thrown into the streets on the perfectly sensible ground that they had been warned. It could be worse of course, the owners of the house could just as easily and with greater gain to their own equanimity hand the intruder to the local militia who forever lurked them in the crowded place where they fish for trouble and abandoned the intruder to their no so tender mercies. Alhassan knew this rule very well, hence the need to stick very closely to Ahmed who had given him a roof over his head. *'But what on earth is Ahmed doing here?'* Alhassan thought. Since his disappearance from the camp, Alhassan had thought that Ahmed had been killed while he was trying to escape. He was dumfounded to say anything to Ahmed.

Ahmed locked the door of the room and they both settled down to do all the catching up.

'What happened?' Ahmed asked.

'Those bastards selected six of us immediately you disappeared. They made us to recite some incantation severally for about twelve hours a day and yesterday they selected two of us from the six and we were told we are lucky to be selected to relocate to paradise. They told us beautiful things about paradise. We were told we would be rewarded with beautiful women with sumptuous eyes. We were told that lot of rewards await us if we kill infidels along with us.'

Ahmed listened raptly without saying a word. Alhassan continued,

'I wanted to ask the commander why he was not taking part in the reward by submitting himself, but on a second thought, I said to myself, this would be an opportunity to escape. If I had asked, they might have killed me. I remembered all your words and the plan we had together to escape, and those words hardened my heart. I pretended to play along with them. My joy knew no bound when I saw you came to rescue me from the shackles of death.'

Ahmed listened attentively as Alhassan spoke. He noticed that Alhassan surreptitiously looked at the shirt and trouser he was wearing but he decided to let the suspense flow.

'I cannot comprehend the reason for all these

senseless killing in the name of Allah,' Ahmed finally said in a low tone.

'Ah, after you left the camp, they brought one Alfa with a very big beard and mustache who came to indoctrinate us. He told us that Allah will have mercy on those of us who run from big sins and all wickedness. He brought out his Koran and read from Sura 53. The Alfa told us that if we die here for the cause of Allah, we were going to have beautiful rewards in heaven. There will be a lot of good things which no persons or angels have seen.'

'Look my friend, I know that if you live a good life here on earth, there is reward for you in paradise. Even the Christians believe the same things but don't tell me you believe that when you kill innocent women and children God will bless you. Most of these people don't confirm those verses from the Quran. You know these guys are always on drugs and they say anything under the influence of drugs?' Ahmed said bitterly.

'How can I confirm those passages when we are not allowed to read the Koran. Only the Alfa opened the Koran and read them out in our presence.'

''I do not believe he was reading the Koran. I am sure they did that as part of their brainwashing scheme. I do not think any holy book will be prosing those puerile acts as a reward. Is that why women are treated like a piece of trash in this country?' Ahmed's anger rose again, remembering how his mother was being maltreated by his uncle.

'I will soon get a Koran and crosscheck these things,' Alhassan grimaced as he said.

'What are you crosschecking?' Ahmed asked in amusement. 'Do you think God will reward with good the killers of innocent and harmless people? These acts are the creation of wicked minds, soon you will tell me that you want to check the Koran if it says we should do suicide bombing. Give me a break, I hope those mad men did not succeed in brain washing you.'

'Brain wash me? No way, my brains are intact!' Alhassan rejoined.

There was a very loud knock at the door. Ahmed and Alhassan immediately kept quiet while the sound of the television was still blaring very loud. Ahmed had deliberately increased the volume of the television to avoid people hearing their discussion. He moved towards the door, peeped through the door hole and saw three men standing at the door. *'Who can these be?'* he mumbled. At a second thought, he stepped back, called the reception on the phone to enquire who the men were looking for. The receptionist rushed to Ahmed's door only to find out that he gave a wrong room number to the visitors. They were looking for the room two doors away from Ahmed's room. The receptionist apologized to Ahmed who refused to open the door to acknowledge the apologies.

Alhassan kept on looking at the cloth Ahmed was wearing. He could no longer bottle the thought in his mind, 'Ahmed, these cloth look exactly like mine.'

Ahmed sighed and replied quietly, 'They are yours.'

'Where is my father?' Alhassan asked anxiously.

'It is a long story,' replied Ahmed soberly.

'Where is my father? Please hide nothing from me!' Alhassan got more anxious.

'We had better sleep now. We have a whole day tomorrow to talk about it.'

'How on earth do you think I can sleep! The commander told me in the camp that my father was a traitor and that they were going to deal with him. Have they dealt with him?' he asked at the verge of tears.

Ahmed had no option but to unfold the sad news to him. Alhassan fell on the bed and cried profusely. The more Ahmed tried to calm him down the more he cried.

There was a knock on the door. This time it was the receptionist. Ahmed opened the door slightly and asked with a harsh tone,

'What do you want?'

The receptionist, feeling so unwanted replied, 'I do not want anything. Just to let you know that your accommodation expires by 12 noon tomorrow. If you wish to stay on, you need to drop a deposit.'

''I will pay it tomorrow morning,' replied Ahmed.

Ahmed sensing he had upset the receptionist, reached his hand into his pocket and brought out a few dollar notes and stretched it to him.

The receptionist with a beaming face, took the money and dipped it in his pocket. 'Nagode, nagode, nagode!' he said repeatedly. But Ahmed didn't wait. He banged the door and shook his head severely. The fare might be the biggest tip the receptionist had got in a long time. This was the biggest tip he had gotten in a long time.

Ahmed turned from the door and saw Alhassan lost in thought.

'So far, there is nothing to show that the terrorist are compromising their opposition to peace in this country. But you never can tell especially with the hideous manner they carry out their destruction. The leaders of these groups, if well judged, are never perturbed by how many innocent blood is shed."

There was no response from Alhassan who only stared into space.

However, Ahmed continued talking, 'Just two days ago some fifty soldiers surrounded a suspected militant hide out in the suburb of MADUGURI leading to fierce gun battle. Two soldiers and over twenty militants have reportedly died from the ensuing gunfight that lasted hours. The suspected gun men reportedly bought a big house in a new housing estate constructed with money from United Nations aids program for developing nations. They were using the house as operational base. Barely a week earlier, Islamic militants in Bornu were attacked by some government troops who tried to rescue three kidnapped women from them on humanitarian aids program serving in Bornu.'

Alhassan stood from the bed, clinched his fist and spoke on top of his voice,

'There is madness in the air amongst us. How can a group of people decide to deny the rest of the world peace? And nobody is doing anything about it? Enough is enough now! I must stop the nonsense going on in the training camp. First thing tomorrow, I will lead the soldiers to that camp!'

'You do not take such decision in a rush,' replied Ahmed.

'What am I waiting for? Until they destroy the whole communities? Please spare me, if I have been out of camp the length of days you have been out, I would take a decisive action,' Alhassan said scornfully.

Ahmed understood his friend was going through some emotional problems, so he decided to be calmed to avoid aggravating the tension. He went into the rest room to allow some rest in the environment. But Alhassan was not done yet, as soon as Ahmed opened the door to come out of the rest room, he continued,

'We need to alert the soldiers tonight. If you are not ready to come with me, I will do it on my own. I know this town very well and I know my way around.'

Ahmed, in a calming tone, replied,

'We need to run to safety before we alert the soldiers. These terrorists have complex network and moles in government circles.'

Alhassan could not take that. He retorted,

'Which safety? Do you think hiding in a hotel is safety?

'But hiding in a hotel has just saved your life from suicide bombing,' Ahmed replied sarcastically.

'What do you call life? Living less than a dog?' Sadam Alhassan barked.

'My friend you have to rest. You have had a difficult day. But Allah be praised that you are still in one piece. If you are going to the police or soldiers to report when you are not free, it is up to you. As for me, I will be leaving here tomorrow for a safe place. If you are interested, you may come along with me. It was your father that gave me the life-line and it is only natural if I extend it to you.'

Alhassan noticed the finality in Ahmed's voice. He had known Ahmed for some time as a very smart guy. The mention of his father woke up something in him,

'My father. You said my father?'

'Yes your father. What I expect from you is how we can sneak to visit your father's grave and pay your last respect rather than embarking on a foolish mission. Who are the sponsors of these terrorist? Who are the terrorists themselves? Before you make a move against this type of people, you must be formidable and well protected and I can assure you, you can only be protected outside this country.'

'When do we go to visit my father's grave then?' Alhassan asked in a surrendering tone.

'We need to go there tomorrow noon when the street is very busy,' responded Ahmed.

'Why should we go there when the street is busy?' Alhassan asked curiously.

'That is the best and only time you can get lost with the crowd. We need to get lost in the crowd to avoid being noticed,' Ahmed said wisely.

'Ah. I now see sense in what you said. That is smart of you.' Alhassan exclaimed satisfactorily.

Around noon on Thursday, 24th March, Ahmed and Alhassan left the guest inn to visit the shallow grave in the compound where Alhassan's father was buried. The compound wore a look of abandonment. They moved to the back of the house and upon seeing his father's grave, Alhassan broke into tears. Ahmed was surprised that the place remained the way he left it. There was no suggestion that anybody entered the place. Alhassan after crying, knelt by the shallow grave, and prayed quietly while Ahmed watched on. The noise from the busy road, as usual, came into the compound. Alhassan finished praying and tried to open the back door when they heard a phone ringing. Ahmed followed the direction of the sound and it led him to the corner of the wall toward the back gate of the compound. He found it. It was a cheap Samsung phone which age is no longer on its side. It rang severally that Ahmed could no longer ignore it. He picked it up to hear what the caller wanted and know who the owner of the phone is.

'Hello! Hello! Mohammed, can you hear me?'

The voice pierced through the phone audibly.

'This is Mustapha, the man the commander told you about. The operation at the Municipal Hotel is 8pm today. We are not going back on the decision because time is running out on us. The federal government are sending anti-terrorist specialist to the city. We must strike before they arrive.'

Immediately he said that, the phone went out at

the other end. Ahmed looked at Alhassan sternly, and shouted, 'There is trouble.'

'What trouble?' retorted Alhassan.

'They want to blow up Municipal Hotel today by 8pm,' replied Ahmed.

'You heard it from the phone?'

'Yes. The man called himself Mustapha and he thought he was talking to one Mohammed.'

'What are we going to do now?' asked Alhassan.

'We are going to do something. I mean something very fast. We need to get back to our guest inn and make some enquires.'

Ahmed and Alhassan moved as fast as their legs could carry them and arrived their guest inn on good time. Immediately, Ahmed started off to work. He called the receptionist and enquired about the Municipal Hotel.

'Where is the Municipal Hotel?' Ahmed asked the receptionist.

'Do you want to go there? It is for foreign people and they are many there,' the receptionist replied. Ahmed eyes shone. He quickly understood why it is a target for the terrorist.

'I don't want to go there to stay. I just want to know where it is located,' replied Ahmed.

'Actually, it is not very far from here but it is off the road. Two streets from here on the left. You need to walk down the street to the end. But let me warn you, the hotel is very expensive,' the receptionist replied, looking at Ahmed strangely,

'You have told me that before. I am not going to stay there but I have to get there to avert a serious disaster,' replied Ahmed. Realizing that he has almost let the cat out of the bag, he quickly tried to make amend,

'I need to catch up with somebody there to pick up some money. It will be a major disaster if I don't get that money. It means I will not be able to pay my bills here.'

The receptionist fell for the lies and encouraged Ahmed to go there quickly, knowing the implication of not getting the money.

'You need to get there very fast. It is not far from here. Go quickly lest you miss the person you are expecting,' the receptionist said like a preacher.

Ahmed told Alhassan to wait back in the rest inn while he took a tri-cycle (popularly called 'Keke' in many parts of West Africa) and headed northward on the main express road that leads to the Municipal Hotel.

As he got to the junction of the road leading to the hotel, he saw a man with a familiar face standing at that junction. He looked closely. It was Omar el Omar, a British trained security guard who worked for Ahmed's father. He was fired by Ahmed's uncle, the next of kin, when Ahmed's father died for perceived disloyalty to him as the new head of the family. Omar el Omar had a stylistic resentment for him due to his hard-liner on religious matters as compared to Ahmed father who practiced the religion with reasons to some extent. He was standing with a bag stuck to his back like a highly trained marksman advancing towards an enemy territory. On sighting Ahmed, he shouted and ran to him. The two of them, locked in each other's embrace, looked very much like father and son who were just seeing each other after a very long absence. Releasing from the embrace, Omar el Omar looked at Ahmed up and down and said,

'You have grown to be a very big boy. How are you? Your uncle told me you travelled overseas to study.'

Ahmed's jaw dropped. 'That is not true!' he shouted. 'We need somewhere private to talk urgently,' he said.

The latter insisted that they talk in in the public instead. However, they had to compromise each other's different view and moved straight to the Municipal Hotel where, to Ahmed's surprise, Omar el Omar was a security attaché. Ahmed told him everything about the camp and the planned terrorist attack that was slated for the Municipal Hotel later in the day.

As a trained security Guard, Omar el Omar planned the security strategy to the minutest details thus laying a trap for the terrorists to walk into it.

At about 7:24pm, the commander drove into the hotel with two young men. At once, Ahmed notified Omar el Omar. At once, a team of anti-bomb officers appeared from the hiding and arrested the three of them. After a thorough search, the bombs were found concealed under the singlet of the two boys while nothing was found on the commander. The bombs were safely demobilized and the three suspected were arrested and detained in the hotel premises for further transfer to the proper place. The commander fixed a dangerous penetrating gaze on Ahmed and muttered,

'You are behind this, eh? I assure you, your days are numbered. We will get you down. Even if I go down now, your days are numbered. From the first day I saw you, I knew you would betray us, you bastard!'

In less than twenty minutes later, a patrol van carrying about four heavily armed men dressed in police uniform arrived the scene and asserted they were on instruction to bring the suspected terrorists. Omar el Omar put a call across to confirm the order, and the three men were handed over to the team of armed police who sped off the hotel premises like demonized people. As Ahmed and Omar el Omar were about driving out of the premises, another team arrived and this time escorted by two trucks loaded with heavily armed soldiers. The team were led by one Captain El Islam. He was very familiar with Omar el Omar. He alighted from the vehicle and they exchanged salutation,

'Where are the bastards?' he asked rubbing his hands on his pistol.

'A team just picked them,' replied Omar el Omar.

'Which team? These guys have outsmarted us again. We have moles inside our system who reveal every move we make against these bastards.'

'I confirmed from the headquarters and I was told to hand them over to the people,' replied Omar el Omar with wide eyes.

'Who did you speak to?' the captain asked curiously.

'I spoke to the commander of the anti-terrorist

unit, I have the conversation recorded " replied Omar el Omar.

'Play it and let's listen to it,' the captain said, looking visibly worried.

The tape was played severally and it was confirmed it was the voice of the anti-terrorist commander. The anti-terrorist terrorist commander, a forty year old Kanuri marksman, is an irrepressible voice of war against terror in Africa and around the Middle East that are ruined partly by religious chauvinism and extremism. He is currently in charge of the anti-terrorism squad in Nigeria. He was trained on counter terrorism from the best academy in Europe and America since he assumed office in Kabul, and he has waged dodged war against the sponsors of terrorism. When the captain heard the very voice of the anti-terrorist commander, he concluded that their lines were bugged. This explains why the terrorists are always ahead of time and in most cases, messages from informants are intercepted and reprisals attacks are done on the informants. The officers left the hotel knowing fully well they have lost this one again. That was not the first one they were losing only that in this case, the terrorists could not inflict destruction on the vicinity.

They have barely taken off heading north-west through the police college —along the major road leading to the outskirts of the city when the weather changed its face, unleashing furious thunderstorms and violent rain drops on the bad roads. The speed of the first car dropped suddenly because the wipers were not functioning thus forcing the other two cars to slow down considerably. They battled to pull through the stormy rain and diverted to an abandoned building and their vehicle came to a halt. People who indulged in the building jumped out from the building into the nearby bush when they saw the soldiers. The soldiers came down from their vehicle, walked straight into the building. Lying carelessly on the floor are marijuana, empty syringes, empty bottles of whisky and cigarettes. They went round the building, entered their vehicle and drove off. Getting close to the major car park where you have thousands of passengers travelling to different locations around the country, the soldiers slowed down. Alas, they were too late because the suicide bombers carried by the commander had been unleashed upon buses loaded with passengers. That was the second time in few months that the terminal would be experiencing this. The explosion led to the mass killing of people~ smoke, wails and cries rented the air. The blast happened twenty minutes before the anti-bomb squad arrived. At least eleven vehicles were affected and six others were completely destroyed. There were reports of several explosions after the first which made the situation apocalyptic. The explosions were followed by billows of black smoke and there was a lot of confusion among people who ran to nowhere in particular. Some of them were with blood on their clothes. Many hawkers and passengers who have not yet boarded a vehicle were all affected and burnt beyond recognition. A lady who managed to escape with only a minor injury, wept uncontrollably when she saw people engulfed in flames inside the vehicles.

The team of soldiers called for re-enforcement and medical first aid to assist those with minor injuries and in few minutes time, siren of ambulance rented the air. The gory site was beyond description. Charred human flesh littered everywhere, and many people were lying dead. Lamentations echoed from the mouth of the survived; which God will take delight in shedding the blood of the innocent, this is murder in the name of Almighty Allah. The anti-terrorist team so far has counted over two hundred bodies being moved for mass burial. Two years ago, explosion of almost the same magnitude at the same park left hundreds of people dead and vehicles destroyed and subsequently a security check point was erected at the entrance but relapsed when the tension reduced.

Meanwhile security agents had condoned off the scene of the attack. Flames from the explosion was still burning while the attackers have disappeared except for the suicide bombers who were used as canon.

Omar el Omar, on hearing the news thought to himself, 'this would have been the fate of Municipal Hotel if Ahmed had not revealed the plot to him. But more worrisome to Omar el Omar was the terrorists' network within the security agents. The terrorists have carefully penetrated the top echelon of the police and army which means since the commander sited Ahmed, his life is in danger. The network of the terrorists has stampeded the local security agencies to abandon the war against terror, but this has made the anti-terrorist squad to collaborate more with the international communities.

Omar el Omar could not hide his deep appreciation for Ahmed's action. He looked at him straight in the face and said, 'I will do everything to make sure you make it to safety. This country is no more safe for you because the commander, as you call him saw you and even went ahead to threaten you. These people do not joke. They mean whatever they say. They are resilient warriors who are guided by false ideological beliefs and are fearless and ruthless in confronting any opposition. The terrorists have many bases and sympathizers. They also have many camps like the one you escaped from where they brain wash many young Muslims who are deceived into believing they are doing the work of Allah.'

Ahmed, looking more confused, asked, 'what is the role of Islam in all these?'

Omar el Omar shaking his head profusely, responded, 'I have said times without number that in the name of Allah, the terrorists and Islam are totally disconnected from each other. These terrorists are under the heavy influence of drugs and satanic rituals. I wonder why they think they are doing Allah's work with satanic sorcery and charms. This is the greatest delusion on earth. Only a dead and powerless god will need charms, bullet and suicide bombers to expand his empire.'

'These people are not Muslims?' Ahmed asked innocently.

'Everybody thinks they are Muslims,' replied Omar el Omar.

'Because they do their acts in the name of God, spilling the blood of the innocent. They even go to the extent of using talisman and charms,' responded Ahmed.

Omar el Omar smiled and replied in a very low voice, 'My son, most people belief that traditional worship belief is inseparable from true religion and again because the Muslims are committed and focused in defense for Islam, they believe that all Muslims are terrorists. The youths are their tools for the execution of their evil works because they of their youthful strength and gullibility. They never debate or question any religious issues. Once the Alfa who is half educated say anything, it becomes a law. Hence in a bid to protect Islam, they drag it to the mud. Finally, because Jihad is highly recommended in Islam, many people presumed that any means to fight the course of jihad is acceptable. They are motivated by the irresistible promises which are very enticing.'

Ahmed looked more confused, 'So you agree that if you kill innocent people, there will be a good reward for you?'

Omar el Omar did not find the question funny because it took him off balance. However he managed to reply, 'the Quran did not say you should kill innocent people. Islam is a religion of peace. When you grow older, you will understand things better. Sometimes, you bring politics into religion to allow a smooth sail of your political idea. The problem is that the politics gives religion a bad coloration.'

'But this coloration will dent the religion and many will misconstrue the religion.'

'When we achieve our aim, we will correct the narration.'

Ahmed became silent for a while. Twice he tried to speak but the words won't articulate. At last, after minutes of silence, he stammered, 'The suicide bombers and their sponsors define what shame and evil connotes.'

Omar el Omar did not respond. However, he felt terrible about the impression created in the minds of non-Muslims and the bastardization of the mind of young Muslims like Ahmed. He was in utter shock and deep sadness about the bad image his dear religion is portraying because of the unreasonableness of his fellow Muslim brothers who are fanatics, who frequently indulge in miscarriage of justice, dispensed without any sense of shame.

The discussion made Ahmed more confused and unearthed a stronger desire to find the truth.

The next day Omar el Omar took Ahmed and Alhassan to the house of one of the senior security officers for safety reasons. This move was a temporal measure to give him enough time to plan their escape to a safer place, most likely Europe where they would be given political asylum. The top security officer lived in a well-protected house with his three wives of which the third and last wife just clocked ten years old few months back. Ahmed could not help wondering why such an innocent child will be forced into such a marriage. His mind became unrest again. He called Alhassan aside on the second day in the house.

'I just cannot understand why our leaders continue to exert force on intelligent and responsible citizens particularly vulnerable and under-aged girls. This is a value system which continues to defile their dignity and undermine their humanity, cutting short their dreams and aspiration, truncating their God given destiny and exchanging it on the altar of lust and avarices of wicked and unreasonable men. For God's sake, how can a man in his fifties marry a girl of ten years old and he was not even ashamed to introduce her to us or was the introduction a warning to us to stay clear? For me, I do not need any warning from anybody to stay clear from an infant. As a God fearing person, I know the difference between good and bad, this case is worse than bad.'

Alhassan did not say a word, he just looked away unperturbed. As they were aside, the senior security officer called both of them to join him in the visitor's sitting room for a brief chat. He tried to make them feel at home because he found out that his two new visitors were always by themselves. Omar el Omar had already briefed him on what the two guys had been through. But particularly he noticed a very high level of resentment from Ahmed while that of Alhassan was indifference. He assumed that the heroic activities of Ahmed must have taken a toll on his behavioral pattern but in the real sense of it the major cause of the resentment was the fact that he was married to a girl who by every standard can best be described as a baby. Ahmed had no regard for the highly respected senior security officer's lifestyle. The few days he had spent in the house, he observed the senior officer was totally morally bankrupt. He caught him molesting one of the maids in the house; he woke up in the middle of the night to discover the scuffle and he hid himself not to be seen by both of them. His heart bleed as the maid cried each time the man raped her.

Few days later the senior security officer threw a party in his house and immediately the guests left, as usual, he pounced on the maid in the house, not minding it was not yet past mid night, the normal time for his uncaught action. This time, the girl resisted and in the process the senior security officer was badly injured and he fell with his hand behind his back. The girl ran to Ahmed for cover, fearing that the worst had happened. Ahmed looked at the innocent girl and said,

'There is nothing wrong in deploying any degree of force in the defense of oneself against an unreasonable assault, particularly coming from an individual who is in a position to understand the full consequence of his action.'

The girl could not respond but continued crying. The officer, to the surprise of Ahmed and the lady, did not react to the action of the girl but went to his bedroom to lick his wounds. This experience began the hostility against Ahmed and necessitated the urgency to get him out of the way by any means. But for the relationship between Omar and the senior security officer, Ahmed would have long been history. Ahmed, later in the day, confided in Omar el Omar who decided to relocate him to the guest house attached to the headquarters for the central intelligence agency located in city central district. At the junction to the Agency, is a gigantic building housing a combined unit of the security agency. The building is guided twenty four hours and only authorized visitors are issued electronic monitored badges, giving them access only to the central reception room where they are met by their host for not more than thirty minutes. The violence in and around the city has necessitated very stringent security measure which in most times cripple business activities due to occasional lock down of terrorist prone areas of the city.

Mustapha Mohammed was destined to be the one that will save Ahmed. He was a charismatic security operative, extremely intelligent and backed by the ruling oligarchy. Unfortunately for Mustapha Mohammed, his sexual escapades are his nemesis.

Although, he isn't pleased with this fornicating act, but he finds it very hard to control his sexual urge. He manages not to trespass in his office but he has many women outside his work circle aside his wives. He barely puts his eyes away from any woman that crosses his path outside his security circle. He thanks his star that this is always shrouded in secrecy. However the greatest irony is that three of the four wives Mustapha Mohammed married are from the security unit. In fact, the last woman he married is from the security unit. His recent wife is very social and domineering. She is one of the most beautiful women in the country, an American trained intelligence officer, very gregarious, one who has so many things in common with Mustapha Mohammed. The other wives on the other hand, are everything Mustapha Mohammed is not. Conservative and reserved; they cannot be described as beautiful but extremely religious.

One Saturday morning, Ahmed woke up with a hangover. There had been a lot of champagne celebration the previous day. He was not used to drinking alcohol. It took him so much effort to get out of the bed. The champagnes were hidden in kettles as though they were water. In a country where alcohol is forbidden, the rich and the powerful get them into the country through corrupt immigration officers and disguise them as water in kettles for oblation. Ahmed was introduced into the circle by his new found friends in the security agency. *That champagne almost killed me,'* he murmured. Never again, he promised himself. He eased his way to the sitting room and checked the time. It was already thirty minutes past the time he will be meeting with Mustapha Mohammed.

'Hunger.' Ahmed groaned, *'This champagne is a hunger fuel.'*

Mustapha Mohammed walked into the room

carrying some documents and a file folder 'Who are you talking to, Ahmed?

'Myself.'

'That is very weird,'

'Yes, you are correct. A lot of water had gone under the bridge in my life.'

Mustapha Mohammed put the documents on the table, 'I brought these documents for you to fill. We have decided to move you to the United States of America for your studies and to keep you safe because the terrorist will not rest until they gun you down.'

Ahmed sat upright at once and felt the hunger disappeared, 'Why are they still after my life?'

'That question is dump. Of course they believe you already know too much. Don't be surprised that they already know you are here. That is one of the reasons we need to get you out of this country to the United States where you will be safer, but not totally safe anyway. For these blood thirsting devils, nowhere is safe.'

'You mean they can still get me in America? Is it no better I die here then?'

Don't get the wrong ideas in your head,' Mustapha Mohammed cautioned, 'Your safety is more assured in America than any other place in the world.'

Ahmed plucked a loose paper from of the forms. It was blank, Mohammed Mustapha quickly took the paper from Ahmed, 'This is not part of your forms. We don't have all the time in the world. Settle down and fill out the forms correctly.'

Omar el Omar took Ahmed and Alhassan to a safe place, after few months of hiding for fear of being killed. Through the help of international agencies a visa was secured for the two boys as refugees to the United Kingdom.

The terrorist camp in Sambisa forest received some visitors from Kaduna state. The commander, as he is generally referred to, was the first to speak,

'We are meeting under the usual rules. No records will be kept, please. This meeting will never be discussed, and we will refer to one another by code names assigned to each location of the country.' There were seventeen men inside the rocky cave in the camp. Four men in plainclothes, armed with AK 47 riffles and bundled up in black overcoat, kept vigil outside. The commander spoke in harsh Fulani accent, 'There is the need to increase the tempo of insurgence in Nigeria, and to achieve this, we need to recruit more people from the Almajiris who are readily available for us here in Nigeria. There is also the need to create general insecurity in this oil rich country and tear it to pieces. The good news is that the politicians are the initiators of this pleasant design so they are willing to work with us and bankroll the project from the loot they get from the country's coffer.'

Sheik Mohammed spoke up, 'How would this promote Islam? It could destroy our great religion in West Africa. It will open up many criticism against Islam.' The sheik is one of the very sincere Islamite whose only mission in the organization is to promote Islam. However, many observers see him as overly sincere.

The bandit leader from Kaduna responded, 'we will make it look like a jihad.'

Sheik Mohammed asked, 'How?'

The commander wanted to respond but the bandit leader was faster,

'We will target churches and non-Muslims. We will condemn everything western. We will fight against education for the girl child and many other things, you know.'

Sheik Mohammed, looking astonished shouted,

'But your daughter is a medical doctor who schooled in America. This is hypocrisy of the wicked order! It is totally...'

The commander will not allow him continue,

'Sheik Mohammed, these are our brothers from Kaduna. They need our help and we must oblige. Time is not on our side,' he said, now facing the rest, 'We will be sending Abdul dogo to Kaduna to turn that state upside down.

'By way of introduction, Abdul dogo is a renowned, deadly and extreme brutal terrorist trainer who has been responsible for many destabilizing acts in different countries. He master minded the assassination of thousands of political leaders in Africa and the killing of many children. His credentials are most impressive and most suitable for a resilient state like Kaduna. As

I speak right now, the Federal government has placed over five million dollars on his life, dead or alive.'

'He is the right person for the Job,' the bandit leader said. 'Can we arrange his movement to Kaduna immediately?'

'He is very expensive to higher. It will cost you one million dollars,' the commander replied.

The bandit leader guffawed,

'Only one million dollars? That is a chicken fee. One of the state sponsors on our side will pay that without a blink. The money our sponsors loot from the state treasuries run into millions of dollars monthly and here we are talking of a meager of one million dollars.'

Sheik Mohammed looked at the bandit leader in utter astonishment and said,

'If this is not about Islam then what is the motives of this unholy action?'

The bandit leader guffawed again and responded, 'Sheik, it is about political power and mineral resources. When we get power, the treasury of the country becomes our private purse and then we can do anything, even promote our religion but first thing first, power. In Africa, power is everything!'

The commander quickly refocused the meeting. They agreed that the money be transferred from Nigeria and paid to an agent in Dubai for onward transmission to the terrorist group. The commander rose,

'The meeting is hereby adjourned. Please observe the usual precautions. No two people should be seen together once you leave this camp. The delegation from Kaduna must observe extra caution in the city and your flights must be booked differently to different destination. The security agents are watching.'

It was a Friday morning, and Abdul dogo, the dreaded terrorist trainer, was having a strategy meeting in a Sambisa forest located four hours' drive from Maiduguri, the capital of Bornu state of Nigeria, where he had no right to be because he came into the country without a passport talk less of an entering visa. He was not alone. He had some people from Sudan, Libya and Mali. Particularly intriguing is the dark skin lady from Sudan, six feet two inches tall, with beautiful shapely breasts and lips that are very irresistible to a man. They call her Aisha.

Unfortunately, in the middle of the forest, Abdul dogo's concentration was distracted by the entrance of several Hilux vehicles carrying all manner of arms and devices.

'Movement into this bloody place is supposed to be restricted and well-coordinated such that there will be no surprises,' he muttered.

'Don't panic. The guys at the edge of the forest sent signals.' Aisha coaxed.

'Me, panic? No way. We run the show here.'

Ten minutes later, Abdul dogo heard another vehicle drive in. A black tinted Prado jeep bullet proof, which had darkened windows that concealed the passengers. This time, he was curious enough to get up and pick his machine gun wielding it carelessly, waiting for the occupant of the jeep to disembark. The door swung open and the bandit leader came out with another taller man wearing a dark shade and a white caftan.

'Hello, my friend,' Abdul dogo said stretching out his hands for a hand shake.

The bandit leader grabbed his hand and responded, 'Very fine.'

He introduced the guest he came with, 'Dogo, meet Dr. Aminu Ahmed, he is one of the top government officials who leaks any plan of the soldiers and police to us,' the bandit leader said, laughing wickedly.

Abdul dogo shook his hand warmly and said,

'You are doing a very good job.'

'We have many of his type in the police and military,' the bandit leader retorted.

'Where is the money? We need to get materials to prepare the bombs for the suicide bombers,' Abdul dogo shouted.

The bandit leader, pointing to the booth of the Prado jeep responded,

'Here we go'

'You mean you put all that money in one vehicle?' Abdul dogo queried.

'Of course, this is American dollar. You can put millions of those wonderful notes in a small box, and besides we are talking of less than a million dollars,' the bandit leader replied.

Behind a shrub ten meters away from where the trio were talking, Gambo Hassan, one of the most notorious terrorists, and topmost on the wanted list of the state security service, was busy trying to rape one of the girls the group abducted two days back when there came a sudden loud noise resulting from the fall of a canister. Gambo Hassan lost his libido out to his instincts as a terrorist. He punched the girl and strangled her to death.

'Throw that trash into the thick forest,' the bandit leader echoed.

'Haba Alhaji, let me see if I can enjoy her a little,' replied Gambo Hassan.

Abdul dogo trying to hide his shock, interjected, 'You mean you are still going to have sex with the dead girl?'

The bandit leader did not wait for Gambo Hassan to reply. He quickly responded,

'Theses dead ones are better if they are fresh. They don't argue or complain how you are doing it.'

'Disgusting,' retorted AISHA. 'Wonders will never end in this country.'

Abdul dogo does not like the Nigerians very much because he has sensed from their action that they are terrible hypocrites unlike the Arabs who are sincere in all they do for ALLAH. The Nigerians are in it for power or for money. Religion is just a means to an end. He could hardly imagine the act he just saw, another part of the crooked lifestyle of the Nigerians. However he has to keep his calm and concentrate on the reason he came to the Sambisa forest. He has trained hundreds of young men for suicide bombing, while the hypnotizing and brainwashing is left for the Nigerians to handle. It beats their imagination as to why all the suicide bombers being trained in the forest are from countries like Chad, Sudan, Mali and Cameron. No single Nigerian is among them. When he asked the bandit leader why there were no Nigerians amongst the suicide bombers, the bandit leader's reply was the greatest shock of his life. He bluntly told him, 'Nigerians are too difficult to deceive. They are not easily gullible when it comes to the game of death.'

It was sunset. The air is very hot, although this place is not very far from the water of Lake Chad. Amid the tall trees are a hardened landscape of dried grasses and small bushes, stud of cigarettes, Indian hemp wrappers of fly-about newspaper pages. A silvery bedding of bullet shells, the remnant of used grenade holders, glitters prettily. This night, the suicide bombers, the bandits and the kidnappers will be deployed to major cities to unleash terror on the citizenry.

'We just received official word from the headquarters. Security will not be tight tonight so the boys can sneak into the cities,' the bandit leader echoed with a jubilant voice.

'How many are we sending tonight?' Abdul dogo asked,

'As many as are ready. Let's make maximum use of this opportunity. We need to bring down this country.'

Abdul Dogo's countenance changed suddenly, 'I have been meaning to ask you this question. What is the objective of this struggle? Is it to bring down the country or to promote Islam?

The bandit leader, as usual, guffawed before replying, 'The aim is to paint the current president weak and incompetent, so that the electorate will vote him out and our person will be voted in. That's what we call fight for power.'

'I now understand...' Abdul Dogo said and paused and started scratching his feet against the ground.

The following night at about twelve mid-night, Abdul Dogo sat with Aisha at the same wooden table in the forest, intermittently chewing groundnuts and flicking his fingernails. At about 1a.m., he saw two rich looking men drove into the forest, and Aisha's heart soared. Both watched as the two men alighted from the jeep.

'Hi,' Aisha mumbled, and pointed towards the bench in front of them while Abdul Dogo reached out for his gun. It is a thing of instinct anytime a stranger comes without prior notice. Abdul Dogo can never be caught off guard.

'Where is the bandit's leader?' One of the men demanded. But Abdul Dogo turned away. It was all he could do to control his anger.

Aisha blinked, 'Huh?'

'Who are you guys?' Abdul Dogo shouted and pointed his gun towards the two men. 'You think you can just walk in here and be asking of anybody without the courtesy of introducing yourself or even responding to our greetings?'

One of the two persons responded,

'My name is Buhari and my friend here is Bala. We work for the bandit leader. We are spies who infiltrate the police to get useful information. We are here to see the bandit leader and let him know we are bringing more of the Almajiri children to be trained. Also, we want to bring to his notice, the potholes in the plan to raid a boarding school for girls and kidnap all the students and their teachers. The Army have anticipated the moves and are planning seriously to tackle us. Again, the hide out where we use as interim place for kidnapped victims is no safe. We need to make plans for another place, and the chief of defense operation for the government is very brutal and uncompromising. The rate at which the government forces are coming after us is becoming frightening as they are taking most of our fighters out and as such we need to lay low until the excitement dies. Let's see if the new general will soft pedal,'

Abdul-Dogo, now facing Aisha, spoke in a very sober tone as if he was regretting the situation in the northern part of Nigeria.

'The Northern region has long faced severe, complex security and humanitarian crises. Since we started our campaign for the right things to be done, they called us terrorists and the bandits. They claimed we went on rampage damaging many communities in the Northern part of Nigeria. They claimed we have unleashed violent extremism due to the high increase and incidences of abandoned children termed, Almajiri. But the real cause of the problem is weak and extremely corrupt governance, embracing poverty thus revealing the vulnerability of the idle youths, and the worsening effects of climate change. The unimaginable violence and crime that have surged over the years transcending national borders and posing significant challenges to neighboring countries like chad, Cameroon and Mali is caused by failure of government. Who are those that have turned Bornu state, Kaduna state, Katsina state and the Lake Chad basin sun regions to be the epicenters of violence and humanitarian disaster?'

Aisha responded, knowing fully the type of response suitable for that question, 'Government.'

Abdul Dogo continued talking, ignoring Buhari and Bala,

'How do you stigmatize a legitimate group fighting a just cause? The press has painted the narrative that the Boko-haram and the bandits have unleashed different forms of violence, armed conflict and criminality of different forms in the north-eastern part of Nigeria in particular and to make it worse they are attributing the loss of lives and displacement of thousands of families to our activities, claiming we pushed them out of their ancestral homes.'

He paused and told Buhari and Bala to go to the next bunker to meet the bandit leader who was in a meeting with other fighters.

He continued,

'It is true that our group has carried out several bombing that have led to the loss of lives and properties worth billions of naira. But what is the reason for that? We must get rid of all the infidels who are perpetuating western education which we vehemently oppose. We must impose Islamic views starting from North East zone of Nigeria. We the Boko-haram group will keep growing as long as the government allows unemployment, lack of good education and high rate of poverty which now remains the order of the day in the north-east and other part of the country.'

Aisha, with concern, asked Abdul-dogo,

'In the midst of these unfavorable condition of living, why is there a very high birthrate?'

Abdul-dogo laughed sarcastically and managed to say as he laughed,

'It is to our advantage. The high birth rate in the Northern part of Nigeria which is directly connected to the polygamous value that is attainable within the Islamic setting and this high birthrate provides an imminent population from which we the *Boko- Haram* recruits them to become members who are fighting for justice,'

He paused and lit a cigarette. Then continued,

'That is why we catch them young. The fighting age of the Boko-haram freedom fighters ranges from fifteen years and above. Because of the non-existence of the basic necessities of life such as electricity, housing, jobs, food and water, the pool of ever increasing population without a commiserate supply of life's need, the crowd of frustrated and fiercely angry young men find themselves in a situation that tends to escalate their adolescent anger into any form of destructive violence and that is the best time to harvest them.'

The bandit leader finished his meeting with the fighters. The meeting was about the plan to attack the Internally Displaced People's camp (IDP). However, the problem is how they were going to pull down the security network in the camp. The security around the camp is very tight,

'Buhari and Bala, you need to proceed to the IDP camp and study the lapses. If we succeed in attacking the camp, we have made a big achievement,' the bandit leader declared.

The IDP camps are located on the outskirts of the city. Several IDP camps exist because most of the villages and towns have been ravaged by Boko-haram insurgency. The camp is managed by the government and guarded by the army and the police. The condition of living in the IDP camp is terrible. It can be described as next to hell. If not for the constant interventions of the private or non-governmental organizations which supply the camp with some basic needs like foods and clothes, the place would have been unbearable for the campers to live. Many of the occupants are being forced to leave the place and migrate other cities and towns where they have family members at great inconvenience. The government had tried to resettle them at the nearest place to their ancestral home but the frequent attack by terrorists makes that plan ineffective. The IDP camps has make-shift shelters for families. The average of nine or ten per household cramped together in one room with an average temperature of 32 degree centigrade. The situation is worsened by the absence or little supply of basic amenities like water, food, clothing, medical care, schools and comforts.

Nearly all the IDPS are plagued with poverty, malnutrition, overcrowding, poor living conditions, and inadequate health care except few who are privileged to be in the good books of the military guards. The camp is prone to several infectious diseases which are highly communicable; Malaria is a trade mark because of the high rate of filth which is a breeding ground for mosquitoes; diarrhea is a common occurrence because of the poor hygiene and acute respiratory disorders. The life in the camp is pitiable. The number of IDP coming up with mental health problems such as post-traumatic stress disorder, depression, and anxiety are numerous. This is basically due to the psychological trauma caused by separation from children and other family members whom they don't know if they are dead or alive- forceful ejection from their homes and the uncertainties they faced in their host communities and IDP camps. When the terrorist strikes, there is commotion everywhere. Parents and family members scramble for safe place. In the process, siblings, children, fathers and or mothers get missing and some are never seen again.

'Never,' shouted the bandit leader. 'If the ladies

are caught, they will sing like parrot. So such mission cannot be handled by ladies.'

At the headquarters of the security high command, the chief of security General Hamza had a brief meeting with one of the senior heads of the undercover police officers in the IDP's camp, a beefy, florid-fierce man. Inspector Musa.

'You are quite right to bring this heinous plan by the terrorists and bandits to my attention,'

Inspector Musa smiled, 'but I am afraid, it is nothing more sinister than trying to beat the terrorists on their game without our traitors getting the hint.'

'I am sorry to have jumped the hierarchy and coming straight to you.' inspector Musa said slowly, rising to his feet.

'Not at all, inspector. It shows you are on top of your job and you know what is happening. When did you say they are likely to attack the IDP camp?

'Next month sir,'

Bala and Buhari entered the camp with the intentions of understudying the potholes as directed by the bandit leader. This camp has over thirty-six thousand people. It was the only safe place in the area yet very hot, full of hunger and death.

'Where are we going to start from?' asked Bala who was already overwhelmed by the population and condition of the people in the camp.

Buhari, who also looked confused, responded in a low tone,

'We need to be very careful. So far, I have counted over forty soldiers armed to the teeth and they are not positioned in one place. And I can still see more of them coming out from different corners of this camp. These people have seen enough trouble. I don't think we should still grind more pepper to their pepper.'

Fear gripped Bala, 'We are meeting under the usual rules,' Bala told him, 'No records will be kept. Put off your recorder. This meeting will never be discussed, and we will refer to one another by code names we have been assigned.'

There were many armed plain clothes security officials bundled up in heavy overcoats despite the very hot weather. They kept vigil outside and inside the camp. The heavy clothing have strong bullet proof. More soldiers disembarked from some trucks and entered the camp. This brought more fear to Bala and Buhari.

Buhari spoke in a hush tone,

'The situation will be a very disturbing news to the bandit leader. This camp is highly impregnable.'

'We need to leave this place immediately before we are suspected,' Bala said in a panicky voice.

'Stop panicking before you put us in trouble,' Buhari said, trying to calm Bala.

It was on a hot Wednesday afternoon. Bala and Buhari walked out of the camp in a frantic hurry because they even entered some places in the camp that they had no right to be. The way they rushed out arouse the suspicion of a secret service police who had been monitoring them since they entered the camp. He was not alone. Some officers had also been alerted of the strange visitors. The officer stopped them while other officers dispersed themselves, ready for any intervention. The officer questioned them,

'What are you both doing here?'

'We are planning to bring food and drugs to the IDP's so we needed to come and do a survey, but we are overwhelmed by the number of people here,' Buhari quickly answered.

'And who is this person with you?' the officer asked.

'He is my brother,' he replied convincingly.

'You want to supply food and drugs to the IDP's. Are you sure?' The officer giggled.

A lady walked past the gate of the camp carrying a plate to go out and beg for food. She was a full fledge lady with a beautiful face. Unfortunately, the officer's concentration was distracted.

'This beautiful girl is begging for food when she has what it takes to live a comfortable life in this camp', he muttered.

He followed the girl and called out to her 'Hey, don't lose your dignity going out to beg for food!' he screamed.

The girl ignored him and walked on. Buhari and Bala took the opportunity to jump into a waiting motor bike and sped past the lady and the soldier. Twenty minutes later another bike stopped. This time around he was curious enough to challenge the bike because bikes are not allowed around the camp.

'What are you doing there?' he shouted.

The bike rider apologized and hurriedly sped off.

He diverted his attention back to the girl,

'What you are going out to look for, I will give you twice free of charge,' he told the girl.

The girl immediately got enticed by the offer. She put up a little smile on her face and he held her hand, caressing it.

Then there was a loud noise from the camp. His libido quickly disappeared and he became suddenly at alert as a soldier that he is. There was commotion in the camp. People scrambled for safety. Nobody knew the source of the sound. The soldiers quickly moved to the direction of the sound but got irritated when they discovered that it was just two electric cables that bridged. The cable coating was peeling gradually and bridging when there was no light. The electricity authority just restored light after seven days, and after the explosion the light tripped off. This means darkness for many more days.

Buhari and Bala found their way back to the forest to meet the bandit leader.

'You people are supposed to be in the IDP camp studying the situation and preparing ground for our attack,' the bandit leader complained.

'This assignment is very important,' Abdul-dogo said. He wondered why the guys abandoned the assignment too.

'What happened?' Abdul- dogo asked.

Buhari waited for Bala to talk, but Bala was not forth coming so he opened up,

'Very well. The situation in the IDP camp is very precarious for any enemy to evade-' he thought of one wit to add, 'Remember – it's very dangerous to throw stones at people if you are in a glass house,' he chuckled and glanced at the bandit leader.

'You are not making any sense.' Abdul- dogo replied looking exasperated and getting angry.

The bandit leader quickly interjected, 'Go straight to the point and stop telling us parable.'

'The situation in the camp is such that you cannot differentiate the security agents from the IDP's because they have so intermingled and deliberately disguised to ward off every attack and prevent any surprise. We were picked out for interrogation. If not for the distraction of a beautiful damsel we would have been apprehended,' Buhari paused, looking downcast and dejected.

'Seriously?' the bandit leader asked sarcastically but continued talking with more authoritative gesture,

'We cannot give up just easily like cowards. We need to re-strategize and do our attack because that will boost our fighters and diminish the government soldiers.'

Buhari was disturbed by the bandit leader's utterance as it was showing vividly on his countenance. Bala was not left out. His heart beat also increased drastically out of fear. But unlike Buhari, he is less emotional and the construction of his heart is never expressed on his mien.

'We need to seek a different opinion from Buhari

and Bala. We have to send different set of people,' Abdul-dogo postulated.

'I think we send ladies this time?' Buhari suggested.

When the door closed behind the inspector. General Hamza picked up a black phone on his desk. 'I have a message for colonel Tunde. We have a big problem, I will explain it at the next meeting. Meanwhile, I want you to transfer more soldiers to the IDP camps. Spread them out in few days, I want them sent out in multiples of twos.'

In the Military barracks, the senior military quarters General Hamza, in his apartment, was awakened in the middle of the night by the ringing of the telephone.

'Who the hell is this person calling at this time of the night?' he yelped. He looked blearily at the bed clock, then snatched up the phone. 'It is two o' fucking clock in the mid night!

Who the----------s?'

A soft crying voice at the other end of the line began speaking, and General Hamza sat upright in bed, his heart beginning to pound.

'They are attacking our village,' the voice came in among the kerfuffle and trying to be as low as possible to avoid the terrorists hearing the call,

'Please speak louder, where is your village,' shouted General Hamza.

'Chibok village. Please send help,' cried the caller.

He replaced the receiver, paced up and down

his room, and redialed the phone calling the radio communication center, the phone was picked at the other end.

'Urgently dispatch the special squad to Chibok village under attack.'

'Instruction taken, action 'the reply came from the other end.

He replaced the receiver, reached over to the bedside table and lit a cigarette. His hands were suddenly trembling. The information of the attack in Chibok is one of its kind. The Special Forces have been depleted due to frequent attacks from the terrorists and the bandits.

'What the hell is going down?' General Hamza asked himself.

At about 11 o' clock. General Hamza picked up the phone and put a call to the theater of war, 'What is the situation report?'

'Operation going as planned, we are in control of Chibok and we are combing the nearby forest to root out the remaining insurgents.'

'Good. Flush out the bastards,' General Hamza gave the marching orders.

CHAPTER EIGHT

The turning points

Like an eagle that flies high above the sky, the years had also flown into the thick air.

Dr. Fatima sat with legs crossed, swindling her seat back and front. She closed her eyes, opened them, closed them and opened them playfully. A broad smile escaped her mouth and gradually parted her lips. So it is true that the dog who eats last eats the fattest meat. God… the once ordinary Fatima is now doctor Fatima!' Now it's time for the mission,' she said aloud to herself. Fatima was fully ready to fight the system which almost destroyed her and marred a lot of bright futures. 'I will hit this system so hard that it will not have strength to destroy our female children again,' she muttered to herself.

Her mind became occupied with the past. How did those who started the fight before her end? Was it not yesterday that she was running for the safety of her dear life when she determined to escape the scourge of child marriage?' Yesterday, she was not sure of her meal or if she would survive the next day? Yesterday, her best friend in the class died during labour because her fragile body could not withstand the rigors of child birth as she was barely over twelve years. Those scars have remained indelible in the chapters of Fatima's heart.

———⇒●⇐———

She walked round the school compound which is now her alma-mater. She had graduated with distinction and only waiting to be given her certificate after undergoing the necessary clearance that qualify her collection of the certificate. It was a beautiful school with wraparound porch and many old beautiful building with ancient designs. 'This school must have been more than a century old,' she reasoned. It was surrounded by sprawling Indiana acreage. She got to her hostel, entered her room- the room she was about to say goodbye to. The room that gave her solace for almost eight years. Fatimah pulled a mug from the cupboard and poured herself a cup of coffee. The comfortable smell of fresh-ground espresso beans and sweet cinnamon filled the air, surrounding her with a million memories. Fatimah looked out of the window and surveyed the yard and the trees and flowers in the compound. A wave of nostalgia swept through her: her primary school in Kano, a thousand wonderful moments; the way they were bound to gather at the details of her and her friends when they are on recess in the primary when all the classmates came out running and doing hide and seek;

the clattering and chattering of her classmates rang in the walls and from the windows.

She took a sip. The thought of her father, her trapped mother and her siblings gushed into her mind. She had neither seen nor heard from them. Her mother was her major concern. As for her father, female children are a means to an end after collecting the bride price, nothing maters. She remembered the case of her eldest step-sister whom her husband maltreated her. Any time the reports got to him, he warned the lady's mother sternly, 'Tell your daughter that I have no money to refund any bride price. It would be better for me if you die in your husband house than to return any bride price.'

Another sip of her coffee and Fatimah couldn't help but cry to let out all her emotions. How many times she had prayed and wished her family was in good condition. Now she is coming to pull her mother and her mother's children out of bondage. Theirs had been a defeated life and always at the center. There has been her father who cared less about his multiple wives and children. He is not an amazing dad. He was very popular for his adherence to strict Islamic views on women, and one of Kano's leading people on Islamic conservativeness. His confidence and ruthlessness spoke caution into every situation. Even after their moms lost their battle to allow their daughters to get mature before marriage, their dad had been a major resistance to the development of the girl child.

It was the first Saturday in September. The season of the year which Fatima didn't like. She called it *the indecisive embers.* She was fully prepared to depart for Nigeria. Her luggage has been neatly packed. She sat inconclusively for the taxi that would take her to the airport. There was still a lot of time left before departure. She was uncertain if she should wait at home or wait in the airport. It was still mid-day. Fatima felt the sadness again in her heart. The way she would always feel it when she thought about her attempted marriage as a child bride by her father. It was hard to imagine how she might have survived that time if she hadn't run away, an action she fanned into a flame with many risk and near death escapes.

She pictured her dad — the man responsible for her travail which has turned out for her good. Greedy, healthy and happy, not caring what befalls his daughters as long as he collects bride price and gifts.

Fatimah took another sips of her coffee, this time barely allowing a gulp to flow down her stomach before taking the next. She also thought about how she had escaped the tragedy of being a child bride. She cannot help but think about the people involved in her success-those who had helped her to achieve her dreams. Her heart cried in gratitude to God and those people she met on her escape route who were benevolent to her. People like Mrs. Williams and Beatrice let the faithfulness of God settle in and around the tender places of their soul. *You've been so good to me, Lord, giving me a love that defines conquest*, she muttered.

Absolutely grateful to God for meeting Mrs. Williams. Fatimah smiled, warmed by the sun streaming through the window and the memories of the past few years. She would forever be grateful to Beatrice for her tenacious love and determination to see her through school and giving her a new lease of life. The best part of her life was when Beatrice adopted her.

Since she met Beatrice, life became very easy for her. For the first time in her life, she felt like a normal person but so much had happened since then, so many seasons and a lot of things have changed. She is now a full grown lady with a degree as a medical doctor ready to confront the world. Now, *what will the coming years look like,* she wondered? How will her father react on seeing her? She knows how her mother will react. For her, it will be an unimaginable joy, palpable brilliant moments of joy, what moments of growth. She thinks about the battle she is about to enter. The heartache ahead which will be a result of her confrontation of the terrible system of child marriage? For a moment, thinking about the possibility of amending and cancelling null and void every barbaric practices of her culture, unknown sorrows seized her heart and brought a rush of fear knowing that changing an old age culture will meet a lot of resistance especially from the beneficiaries of the system.

Fatimah exhaled heavily and moved towards the window to grasp some fresh air. Suddenly, the feeling of fears fade as quickly as they had come. There was a rush of stubborn vigor and vehemence and she spoke out with a very loud voice *'I must succeed whatever the future holds. I must overcome!'*

Fatimah glanced at her wrist watch. The time for her departure was fast approaching and the airport was about thirty minutes' drive. Just then the taxi drove into the compound and Fatimah moved all her things in to the taxi. *'Off to the airport,'* she shouted in joy.

—————————

The plane landed successfully at the Murtala International Airport, Lagos. Fatimah was welcomed into the country by Beatrice and one young lady from an NGO which kicks against gender violence.

'Welcome back home, my daughter!' Beatrice said in excitement, giving her very tight hug. There was a moment of passion between the two ladies. Tears of joy was rolled freely from Fatima's face. Beatrice tried to control her emotion, remembering suddenly that she has forgotten the lady she came with. She turned quickly to the lady,

'Please meet my daughter, Fatimah. Fatimah this is Dr. Joyce Jephat. She is the initiator of the NGO which fights against gender violence. She is the lady I spoke to you about while you were in the Uk. You will be doing your National Youth Service with them.'

Fatimah reached out and gave Dr. Joyce a cheek kiss and hug.

Twenty minutes later, they were all seated in a chauffeur-driven Prado jeep, heading to Beatrice's house. Fatimah stared out of the car window, 'Look,' she exclaimed. 'Lagos is getting more beautiful!'

Beatrice looked at Dr. Joyce in uneasiness and laughed sheepishly at her, 'You are still in the airport vicinity, girl. Reserve your comments until you get to the city Centre where you see dirt littered everywhere with the massive noise pollution.'

The vehicle sped past the roads and Fatimah realized that things have not really changed but rather had gone from bad to worse. Coming from United Kingdom where everything seems to be in order to a disoriented environment where nothing seems to work brings a kind of sorrow to her heart. Many questions begin to fill her mind. *What is the government doing with the oil and gas revenue? What about the taxes people are paying?* She could not fathom the degree of neglect by the government. Sadly, the north she is from is far worse when she remembers the Almajiris and the abandoned girls in the hospitals due to one ailment or the other resulting from infant pregnancies.

'Oh what a country,' she exclaimed.

Beatrice turned to her, 'my daughter, what is wrong? Please take it very easy. You are back to contribute your quota to nation building, remember.'

'The rot is unbelievable. You mean the airport vicinity was just a façade,' Fatima responded.

Beatrice chuckled,

'My daughter, you are just opening your eyes. In this country, there is no power supply. Everybody generates his own power through electric machines. There is no water supply too. Everybody provides his own water. You pay tax and other government pay for nothing. All the money is embezzled. This explains why millions of Nigerian youths are fleeing the country in droves and the government doesn't even give a damn.'

The vehicle came to a halt in Beatrice's home. The occupants rushed out of the house. Everywhere was filled with joy. Old acquaintances, renewal of old ties, hugs and kisses filled the air. The neighbors rushed into the house to see how the timid rural Fatima has been transformed into a posh sophisticated beautiful medical doctor with very good command of the English language mixed with a bit of British accent.

Beatrice and Fatimah had been seated in the living room with some other guests for just few minutes when Mrs. Williams came in from outside where she was standing with Mr. Williams who deliberately refused to come into the house. Fatimah stood up to hug Mrs. Williams who equally gave her a warm embrace. They locked in each other's grip, muttering and pouring out emotional gosh.

Mrs. Williams sat next to Fatimah and playfully asked about her experience in the UK. She acknowledged her beauty and her growth. Beatrice surreptitiously eyed Fatimah in admiration.

'You should see the neighborhood and greet some of your old friends and your teachers,' Beatrice told Fatimah with enthusiasm. 'Your old cantankerous teacher has not been feeling well. I told her you were coming today. She wanted to go with us to the airport but her health did not permit her.'

Mrs. Williams laughed and everybody else laughed at Beatrice description of the teacher.

'I think what you meant to say is that the teacher is a talker,' Mrs. Williams opined.

They all watched as Fatimah and Beatrice exploded into laughter. The laughter was an experience only two of them understood. Others were at a loss. Some years back, when Fatima was in secondary school, the teacher brought Fatimah home from school and started conversing with her but suddenly she bit her tongue and surprisingly she continued talking not minding the pain. Beatrice told her to be quiet and treat her mouth which was partly full of blood but she replied, 'If I close my mouth the pain will be more.'

When the laughter subsided, Mrs. Williams asked, 'What is wrong with the teacher?'

'She has a pain in her throat,' replied Beatrice.

'I am sure she overstressed her vocal cord due to much talking.'

'You can't rule it out because talking is her hobby,' Beatrice commented.

Fatimah, laughing very loud, spoke in an accented tone,

'When she was my teacher, she talked from the beginning to the end of the lesson. No other person was allowed to talk in the class.'

They visited the teacher on that same day Fatimah returned. She was elated and tried to speak. Beatrice beckoned her not to talk but she managed in pains to mutter some words,

'Welcome my child. I knew that you will make it in this life.'

She wanted to continue talking but a sharp pain held her in the throat and she held her neck with deep pains in her eyes. Mrs. Williams looked very worried, 'Please stop talking. We understand how you feel.'

It was a brief visit. The teacher was prayed for and the women went back home.

CHAPTER NINE

The struggle, the fight

Dr. Joyce had meeting with Beatrice and Fatimah and decided to post Fatimah to Kano to do her service with the NGO because that was a familiar terrain for Fatimah knowing she hails from Kano. Again, it would be a source of inspiration to young and adult females when they see what beautiful and successful woman Fatimah had turned into. The presence of Fatimah will challenge the status quo in Kano.

There might be other sounds, they were not just loud and clear like the rustling of the leaves on tress as result of the cool evening breeze. Dr. Amina's eyes glistered with surprise. *'Who can that be?'* she said under her breath. These days, she hardly received visitors after the police encroached her house and arrested her for keeping three underage girls without their parents' consent. Those girls were about to be married to men old enough to be their grandparents. It was a coincidence that three of them, who were from different homes, came to her house at the same time.

Dr. Amina has just finished her bath when the knock on door started. She tarried, thinking it was another harassment from the police but the knock continued unabated. Hurriedly, she put on her clothes and walked to the door. Although, she was scared of the harassment, she had already conditioned herself to it. She opened the door slowly,

'Yes, what can I do for you?' she asked with a stern look.

'Good evening, Ma.' the stranger said energetically.

This voice is familiar somehow to me but the accent is totally new, she thought, and frantically looked on at the stranger at the door.

'It is me Fatimah!'

Dr. Amina was now able to place the sound of the voice and the face although time had made some adjustment on the personality but it matched. 'Oh my God! Is this you, Fatima? Aliamdulilai!' she shouted in excitement as she wrapped Fatima in her arms.

It was another emotional reunion. Fatimah slowly narrated her ordeal and how she survived to Dr. Fatima who also listened with rapt attention. She started from how she fled from Kaduna down to Lagos and finally to the United Kingdom then back to Nigeria, Kano eventually.

'This is highly unbelievable!' Dr. Amina exclaimed.

'Your story must be published by the tabloids. When you settle down, we will address a press conference,' she paused and thought for a while before she continued,

'God brought you back as a nemesis to the enemy of the society.

'Have been to your home to see your parents?' she asked compassionately.

'Ah no. I need to be properly prepared before I see them' Fatima replied.

'Where are you staying?'

'The NGO gave me accommodation in the Government Reserved Area.'

'That is very good. That area is very well secured.'

'Who does the NGO advocate for?'

'They rehabilitate abandoned infant mothers and their children especially those infected and whose body systems have been destroyed due to pregnancy at infantile stage.'

'That is a very good place of service for you,' Dr. Amina said in a very pleasant and satisfactory tone.

'I am one of the happiest persons in the world having seen you today after a long while!' Dr. Amina said happily. She walked into the kitchen to serve her some food.

After Fatima's visit, sleep left Dr. Amina. It's 3am already. Her mind wandered through the past. 'Yes, it's right. It's just right,' she told herself constantly. What Fatima had passed through in life made her a warrior. And a very good warrior at that. However, it was a hard life for such a tender age at that time.

Immediately the clock struck 5am, she slipped out of her bed, and dialed Pwajok's number, but Pwajok didn't pick the calls. She was furious. 'Why would Pwajok not pick her number by this time?' she said under her breath. She tried to accept that he was still sleeping. She slid back to her bed, closed her eyes to catch a little sleep.

She was barely sleeping when the phone started buzzing. Grudgingly, she picked the call.

'Hello' the rough sound came from the other end of the phone.

'Good morning, Pwajok,' she murmured.

'I missed your call, please.'

'Yes. Guess what?'

'You know I am not good at guessing.'

'Okay. You remember that brilliant girl, Fatima, we took to Kaduna?'

There was a pause at the other end.

'Are you there?' Dr. Amina asked in exasperation.

'Yes. I am trying to figure out who the Fatimah is. I remember vividly that we took we took three girls to Kaduna. But I don't know which of them you are talking about.'

'I am talking about the light skinned beautiful girl that the police men came searching for at two different times. Can you remember now?'

'I remember her now, that bold girl?

'She is now a medical doctor and in town now.'

'I can't believe that! You mean that girl is now a doctor? How did she do it?'

'It is a very long and bitter story that ended very

sweet. I cannot tell you on phone. When you come to my house, you will get the full gist.'

'I can't wait for the story. This is a very good news and our organization can use this story to push our case.'

'Yes, I have already told her.'

Truly, Fatimah was destined to be great. She became very charismatic and highly respected by the public. Everybody wanted to meet with her to the extent that other non-governmental organizations started showing interest in her and appointing her as the team leader to sensitize young girls on the need to go to school.

Often, when there were gatherings, unavoidable occasions where children gathered in the city center for one celebrations or another, Fatima and other like minds would be invited to speak to them.

Fatima hasn't gone home to see her family. There is only the news which has spread like wild fire even to her parents' house that there is a young woman who has become the latest topic among households and villages. However, none of her family members do not give it a thought that it is Fatima.

She finally decided to visit her parents and siblings. Not wanting to go alone, she invited Dr. Amina and Pwajok to go with her.

It was a hot Saturday afternoon. Fatima shakes her head as she tries not to compare the weather to the ones in the State. Although, there were times when the weather would not be so kind, but it's not always as sunny as this. A black Prado drove into the unfenced compound. There were many unkempt children who lingered outside the house playing on the hot sand.

Fatima and her entourage alerted from the jeep. An elderly woman jumped out of a room in building on sighting the visitors and their vehicle. The elderly woman called out Fatimah's father that there are visitors asking for him. The old man came out with three other women presumably some of his wives. Fatimah noticed that her mother was not among them.

Fatima was not recognized by any of the people that came out including her father. There was a suspicious silence until the man of the house broke the silence,

'What do you people want?' he spoke in Hausa language with no pleasantries or any sign of welcome.

'We are looking for Mama Fatimah,' Dr. Amina was saying when Mama Fatimah walked out of the house and her gaze caught Fatimah. She looked at her sternly and suddenly gave a loud cry,

'Fatimah! Fatimah is that not you?'

At once, all eyes turned to Fatimah's direction. Her father was shock and disbelieve. With excitement, Mama Fatimah grabbed Fatimah, almost compressing her. 'Fatima, oh my Fatima,' Mama Fatima said with tears as she kept on embracing her daughter. Her siblings also jumped up and down in excitement.

'One would think I am already dead by the way you're all acting,' Fatimah's father looked at her in utter shock when she spoke those words with the *oyinbo* accent.

'I have waited patiently for a time like this that we will all gather and I will talk to you, Papa,' Fatima paused and looked at everyone who also fixed their gaze at her in disbelieve.

'I know—' she continued, 'that I have shocked you. But I am happy that I am alive and successful for you to see how life should be for a girl child.'

Fatimah stopped and gave them all a few minutes to digest what she had said.

'We wanted the best for you based on our tradition and not to punish you,' her father said, trying to avoid Fatima's stern look.

'Our tradition on underage marriage is retrogressive, oppressive and should be declared as child abuse and a crime against humanity. This tradition is not helping the young girls. In fact, it kills their dreams, and buries their talent. This practice must stop.'

There was an awkward silence. Fatimah's father stood in awe and could not believe that this is the same Fatimah he was commanding around and pushing here and there. The whole family except the mother has this sudden fear for her new status.

'This is not the time to be sorrowful. Let's forget the past hurt and thank the Almighty Allah for preserving our daughter,' Fatimah's mother said as she rushed to get some chairs for the visitors.

Fatima's father, with fear, apologetically told the visitors that the room inside cannot accommodate them and told them to sit under the big mango tree in the compound.

Mama Fatima assisted by Fatima's siblings carried the chairs under the trees.

'Hey, Abudul. Big head,' Fatima called out at her little brother as he tried to stay aside from the mango tree. Abdul, who had wanted to greet Fatima like that before, wasn't sure whether to play with her or not as he saw that she is now a big girl. It was their way of greeting each other when they were little. 'Fatty, Fatty. Small head!' he responded with great joy and ran back to embrace Fatima.

All the members of the family and some other outsiders gathered under the tree. While some sat, others stood because there wasn't seat again to sit on. Dr. Amina took the floor and narrated the travail of Fatimah to everybody and delved into the dangers and consequences of under aged marriage. For the first time, Fatimah's father was humbled on the subject matter. The success of Fatimah has intimidated him into submission.

Soon, it was Fatimah's turn to speak. She spoke fluently and contributed immensely to Dr. Amina's speech. She shed more light into the danger of child marriage and explained how the society is losing from killing the dreams and destinies of young girls. Using herself as an example, she says,

"Today, I am a medical doctor. The first medical doctor from this community and the first medical doctor from this large family. I am standing before you today because I rejected marrying as a child. Now, I have gone to school, I have achieved my dreams. Now

I can marry. Papa, can you see that there are stages to life?'

There was a loud applause from everybody showing signs of approval. Fatimah's father was immediately captivated with his daughter, Fatimah. In a joyful mood, he started speaking in Hausa, 'Nagode Allah, Allah Nagode!'

Fatima's high attainment and enlightenments on child marriage changed a lot of mindset.

The only major challenge some parents have is that they have no money to sponsor their female child to school. Poverty now a major issue in the community concerning the girl child education.

A Mallam who confronted Fatimah said, 'Rather than leave the girl child at home to become wayward it will be better they get married.'

But Fatimah replied, 'Rather than marrying out a child because you have no money to send her to school, why not send her to get a skill like cloth making, catering and any other trade.'

The Mallam exclaimed, 'Yauwa.' It was a response that shows agreement to the speaker's point of view.

Fatimah continues her crusade against under-aged marriage unabated. She has written to the government agencies seeking permission to address schools to educate them on the dangers of child marriage. In some cases, she got the cooperation and in some cases she was highly resisted.

EPILOGUE

'Hello,' the narrator says as he fumbles with the mask on his face, 'so you see, what has been happening behind the veil is now unveiled. The scourge of child marriage and the Almajiris systems have been dealt a fatal blow. The lion can now eat straws like the ox.'

GLOSSARY OF TERMS

Baka tarbiyyantar da 'yarka da kyau: You did not train your daughter.

Tsohuwa: Old woman.

Yah allah: Oh God.

Omo onile: The child of the landowner.